# The
# Cone Stories

A Collection by
Stuart Real

Illustrated by
Danielle Manning

Real Books For Children

Daniel
lets hope you
never grow up.
x

**The Cone Stories**

**A product of
Real Books For Children**

First published in Great Britain by
Lulu Publishing

Copyright © Stuart Real 2007
Illustrations Copyright © Danielle Manning 2007

ISBN 978-0-9556755-0-8

For Lyn,
Without your crazy ideas none
of these stories would have
been born.
Thank you, I love you so much.

For Danielle,
Thanks for all of your hard work.

And for Zak and Kyle,
Thank you for believing!

# Contents

# Cones

Have you ever been a passenger in a car and seen hundreds of orange and white cones lined along the motorway slowing all the traffic down?  Have you noticed the cones only ever slow the traffic down when you are in a hurry to get somewhere?  Did you think that the workmen who mend the roads placed them there?

Well, maybe the workmen do put them there or maybe there is a different reason.  Perhaps the truth is, the cones you see in the motorway all have a mind of their own.  They stand on the motorways just to cause traffic jams because they are naughty, in fact they are very naughty.

In a motorway maintenance yard close to the M4 the manager was locking the gates.  Inside the yard were thousands of orange and white traffic cones all stacked on top of one and other.  There were piles of grit for when the roads became icy and lots of different vehicles.

Colin, the largest of the cones, one with an orange flashing light on his head, jumped down from his place on top of one of the piles and stood in front of all of his friends.

"Do you know what day it is?" he asked.

"Friday," the others replied.

"It's not just any Friday," Colin said. "It's the Friday before bank holiday weekend."

"So?" Keith, the smallest and youngest cone asked.

"So, it means we can have lots of fun and slow down all the traffic for the whole weekend," answered the large cone, there was a sparkle of mischief glinting in his eyes.

Colin marched up and down in front of the ranks of cones and told the tale of the huge traffic jam back in nineteen ninety-eight.

His uncle Charles had brought the whole of the M4 to a standstill over a bank holiday weekend. He told them how his uncle had planned it for months when he stood out in the snow and rain during the winter on the motorway. The news reporters at the time said that "Essential road repairs" caused the hold ups. But Colin knew better.

"I know we can do it too," said Colin proudly, puffing out his chest. "Only we will do it better."

"Don't be so silly, Colin," Grace the gritting lorry said, as she awoke from her long summer sleep. "It is very naughty."

"Yes I know," Colin said with a laugh. "Now, who's going to help me? It will be so much fun. Like me you must be bored with sitting round this yard waiting for something interesting to happen."

"We are," chorused all the cones.

"Then join me."

"We will!"

"I really don't think you should be doing this Colin, the manager will be very cross with you," said Grace quite sternly.

"What do you know?" answered Colin. "You sleep all summer long, you only work in the winter and spray people and cars with grit. You have loads of fun whenever it snows or is icy. We're all bored."

Within minutes thousands of cones had crammed themselves into Lance, Leonard and Leslie the three lorries that lived in the yard. Vera and Valerie, two box vans were full of cones too. Even Simon, Scott, Suzie and Sally the "Sorry for any delay" signs were sat in the back of the vehicles waiting to go out onto the motorway.

"How are we going to get out of the yard?" Leonard, the largest lorry asked.

"Easy," replied Colin. He was sitting in Leonard's passenger seat. "All you've got to do is barge through the gates and the old rusty lock will break."

Leonard began revving his engine. His tyres squealed as they spun on the wet concrete and he sped forwards towards the gates.

Suddenly there was another loud squeal as the tyres of the other two lorries skidded on the wet floor and chased after him. There was a loud thud and crash too. Grace had parked herself in front of the gates. All of the cones lurched forwards and smacked into the front of the lorry, a few even fell out of the back. They jumped out of the way before they were squashed under the great rubber tyres of Lance, rushing up behind.

"Get out of the way!" Leonard shouted. "We've got a job to do."

"I'm not going to let you pass," yelled Grace. She tried to stop herself from shaking nervously. "You are all being naughty, very naughty indeed." Grace did not want to spoil anyone's fun, but she knew causing traffic jams is very naughty. The cones and all of the vehicles in the yard were her friends and standing up to friends is much harder than standing up to bullies.

Leonard revved his engine once again and his wheels spun on the concrete in a deafening screech as he tried with all his might to push Grace out of the way. It was no use she was as strong as an ox, or a huge gritting lorry with her brakes on. Lance and Leslie had to push too before Grace started to slide slowly backwards. She crashed into the gates and they fell off their hinges. The lorries pushed so hard she fell into a ditch next to the grass verge with a huge sloppy splodge as she landed in the smelly mud.

"Sorry, Grace," said Leonard, as he rushed past. "We have got a job to do. I hope we haven't hurt you."

The cones were free.

The five vehicles charged through the broken gates and raced along the motorway.

"What do we do now?" asked the cones.

"When we get to the start of the motorway I want you all to get out one by one and line yourselves up on the grass in the middle of the road. Big Carl from the M5 depot is going on the same mission tonight. All of his cones will stop the traffic on the M5 too." Colin paused for a moment, then he puffed out his plastic chest and proudly said. "This will be much better than Uncle Charles' try."

At the end of the motorway the five vehicles turned around and began their journey back along the M4 towards Bristol, the cones began jumping out of the lorries and vans and started lining themselves up on the grass between the two carriageways.

By midnight all of Colin's and Big Carl's cones were in position. Messages were passed up and down the lines, which stretched from London to Bristol and from Bristol to Birmingham. They were to stay in position until sunrise, then they would all run onto the road and cut it down from three lanes to just one.

The sun began to climb in the sky, sunlight was shining through the trees and across the fields. All of the cones dashed onto the motorway and into position. By nine o'clock there was a ten-mile queue on the M4 and a seven-mile queue on the M5. By ten o'clock the queues had trebled.

The manager of the motorway maintenance yard had phoned the police at eight o'clock, when he first arrived at the yard to report all of his cones, three lorries and two vans had been stolen and his gates and gritter were damaged. The police still hadn't arrived by eleven o'clock because they were all held up on the motorway with the rest of the traffic. The towns and villages around the two motorways began filling up with cars too as the drivers tried to find a new routes avoiding the motorways. By lunchtime both of the motorways were completely blocked, the queues had even spread onto the M25. People couldn't get to the airports and missed their flights. The whole country was in total and utter chaos.

It took nearly three weeks for all of the cones to be collected and taken back to their yards. In that time thousands of deliveries were not made, food went off and parcels weren't delivered. Colin sat in his shed back at the yard near the M4 and smiled to himself.

He had beaten his Uncle's record. Uncle Charles had only managed to stop the traffic on one motorway, Colin had done it on two and a bit of a third one. He was a hero around the maintenance yards up and down the country every cone knew his name. He had already begun planning next year's adventure. Maybe he could stop all the traffic in the whole country next time. He let out a long contented sigh and fell asleep. The large cone with the light on is head started to dream about traffic jams all over the country and how much fun he could have causing all those hold ups.

Whenever you are next sat in a car on a long journey have a look out of the window and see if you can see any naughty cones lurking at the side of the road waiting to cause trouble in the morning. If you do see them waiting, tell them to stay where they are and not to be naughty. If the cone's light is flashing then tell Colin not to plan any more traffic jams, because that is naughty too. Sometimes workmen really do put cones on the road to stop accidents happening at roadworks. When you see these cones all stood in a line doing their jobs please give them a smile and a wave to cheer them up and stop them getting bored. If they don't get too fed up then, hopefully, they won't cause any mischief.

# Runaway Cones

Have you ever seen dirty, orange and white traffic cones in strange places?  Have you ever wondered how they got there?  Have you wondered why they were there?

Sometimes they appear in the middle of a field or in a stream.  Sometimes they are just standing or lying at the side of the road alone.  I bet you thought that people left them there didn't you?  Sometimes people do just leave them there, but sometimes they are there for a totally different reason.

It was a cold winter morning in the motorway maintenance yard close to the M4.  The sun hadn't even begun to climb into the sky when Colin and the other cones heard the jangling of keys and the lock on the huge rusty gates being opened.  The manager of the yard pushed open the gates and wandered around the yard blowing into his cupped hands to warm them up.  It was so cold the cones could see the breath of the manager spiralling from his nose like smoke spiralling from a dragon's nostrils.  Two more workmen parked their cars outside the gates and joined the manager.  He mumbled something to them the cones could not hear from their shed.  One of the men walked over to where Leslie, one of the lorries, was sleeping, opened his door and climbed in.  After a bit of a cough and splutter Leslie's engine roared into life and the old, dirty lorry drove round to the front of the yard.

"Tea is ready," called the second man from the hut's doorway.

"Now coming," replied the driver.

When all three men had gone inside for their tea Colin leapt down from the top of the stack and tiptoed over to the lorry sat in front of the shed. "What's happening?" he asked.

"I don't know. I think they said something about spending all day mending kerbstones on the A-road," the old lorry replied.

"What does that mean?" Snapped Colin. He thought it sounded boring.

"A few cones standing around in the cold all day and that's about it really," answered Leslie.

Colin was nearly right, it didn't sound a bit boring. It sounded completely boring.


When the men had finished drinking their tea and munching on biscuits they came back into the yard and began loading cones onto the back of Leslie. Actually, the two men loaded cones onto the back of Leslie while the manager barked orders to them from Leslie's warm cab where he was sitting fiddling with the radio. He wanted to find a proper radio station to listen to, one that doesn't play new fangled music.

"Forty cones should be enough, just the little ones we won't need the ones with lights on top we should be back before dark. You'll need some tools and a stop go sign as well," the manager shouted over the top of the noise of the radio blaring across the yard.

"No cones with lights on," Colin muttered and moaned under his breath in disgust, when he heard the manager's orders. "How am I going to cause mischief on the roads if I'm stuck in here all day?"

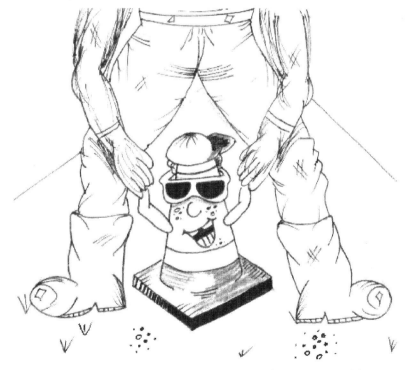

Keith the smallest cone just laughed at the grumpy old cone when he was carried to the back of Leslie. "Bye bye, Colin. I hope you have a good day."

"Humph!" snorted Colin.

After a short journey the cones were lined up along the white lines in the middle of the road and the manager stood in the middle of them holding the stop go lollipop sign, every now and then he would twist it so it faced the other way and the traffic could move off.

"This is boring," Keith whispered to Katie, who was stood next to him. "Do you want to go and find some fun?"

"Where?" she replied, whispering as quietly as she could. "We can't just leave the side of the road, the men will see us going."

"When they stop for lunch we'll make a run for that hedge and go and have some fun. We will be back before they pack up and leave."

"Promise?" asked Katie.

"I promise," replied Keith.

Just before the men stopped for lunch they shoved the pole of the stop go sign into the hole at the top of Christopher. They tied some string to either side of it so they could sit in Leslie's cab, eat their sandwiches and still turn the sign from stop to go whenever they needed to.

"Now is our chance," whispered Keith and he hopped to the

hedge. Katie followed close behind.

The two cones dived into the hedge. As soon as they had entered the hedge they saw the deep ditch behind it. It was too late and they both slipped and slid into the ditch, they landed head first in the thick smelly mud at the bottom.

"This isn't any fun at all. I don't know why I listened to you," moaned a muddy, upside down Katie.

"It's got to be more fun than standing in the middle of that boring road all day long," replied Keith. "Now come on, try and stand up then we can make our way out of this ditch."

The smelly mud squelched and slurped as the two naughty cones tried to pull themselves out. After a few tries the mud eventually went schloop and they were free. They struggled and scrambled up the bank on the far side of the ditch and stood at the top. They were on the edge of a field, a field full of cows.

"I'm scared, Keith, those animals might eat us," Katie said. She trembled as she stared at the cows.

"They won't eat us, they are cows."

"They're what?" asked Katie. She was still very scared.

"Cows. They only eat grass, they won't eat two plastic cones."

"Where do we go now?" asked Katie, still keeping an eye on the scary cows. "We can't get back up the other side of that ditch it is a lot steeper and wetter than this side."

"Let's head across the field and see what we can find," said Keith, as he began hopping through the grass and in between the legs of the cows.

The two cones hopped across the field and through a gate at the far side into another field. They hopped across the second field and through a hedge. After hopping across two more fields and through two more hedges Katie was getting worried.

"We are never going to get back to Leslie on time now," moaned Katie.

"Never mind, we'll just have to walk home."

"But we don't know where home is," sighed Katie. "We're

lost."

"We're not lost. Lost is when you don't know where you are," said Keith. "We know we are in this field, we just don't know where this field is."

Katie started to cry, the tears left long streaks of orange under the mud.

"Don't cry. We will get home. Hopefully."


It started to get dark, Keith and Katie had not found their way home. The workmen, Leslie and the other cones drove into the yard. The cones were unloaded and put back into the shed. Leslie was parked around the back. The men left and the manager locked the old rusty gates.

Colin jumped down from the top of the stack. "Did you have fun standing in the middle of the road all day Keith?"

There was no answer.

"Keith? Keith where are you?"

"Keith and Katie ran off into the hedge when the men weren't looking," replied Clive. He loved telling tales and getting the other cones into trouble.

"Where are they now?" asked Colin.

"I don't know," said Clive. "They never came back."


Three nights went by before Keith and Katie appeared

outside the locked rusty gates of the yard. They were tired and dirty, Keith's white shinny plastic cover was torn and trailing along behind him. When the manager turned up and unlocked the gate he bent down and picked them both up.

"Where have you two been? What are you doing out here? Sometimes I think you cones have got minds of your own," he muttered.

He didn't know that they had. He placed them back in the shed on top of one of the stacks and went to put the kettle on.

"What have you two been up to?" Colin asked angrily, whilst getting down from the top of his stack and folding his arms across his chest.

"We've had an adventure," replied Keith, his eyes opened wide with excitement. "We've slept in barns, ran across cow fields. We waded across a stream and caught a lift from Tony, a big friendly green tractor, and one night we even had to sleep on top of a shed because a dog was trying to chew on us, that's how my white cover got all torn. It was so much fun, you should have come with us."

"I wouldn't want to come with you, it sounds boring," replied Colin, lifting his nose into the air. "I had much more fun here at the yard."

"Doing what?" asked Keith.

"Er, um, well I," answered Colin. "Look at your tatty white

cover, go and get a new one straight away!"

Keith hopped towards the door and passed Katie and her mother.

"You're a very naughty girl, running off like that. It could have been dangerous," said Katie's Mother.

"It was dangerous, Mum," Katie snivelled. "I promise I'll never run away again."

"I will, it was so much fun," said Keith to Katie's Mother. He then turned to Colin and shouted, "I'll tell you all about our adventure when we go out to work today."

"Humph!" snorted Colin.

If you ever see a dirty, torn, orange and white cone

somewhere where it shouldn't be, like in a farmer's field or on top of a shed, don't worry. Keith goes on lots of adventures, he is always trying to find his way home. Sometimes some of his friends join him just to see if adventures are as much fun as he says.

As for Katie, she has never been on another adventure. She is a well behaved little cone who does as her Mother tells her and stays well away from trouble.

# Frozen Cones

Have you ever been a passenger in a car on a cold winter day and seen gritting lorries spreading grit over the roads? I bet you thought they were spreading grit to stop the cars and lorries slipping on the ice and causing accidents. I also bet you thought the gritters were spreading grit for the safety of the rest of the vehicles on the roads.

Most of the time gritters are there for the safety of other vehicles. Sometimes the gritters are spreading grit for a totally different reason.

It was a cold and wet winter day on the M4 motorway. Colin and all his friends were out on a job, a long job. They were stood along the side of the motorway to protect the workmen as they repainted the white lines. There wasn't much traffic on the roads, Colin and Keith were bored because there were no queues of traffic in jams to laugh at. Colin decided to play a game to stop the boredom.

"I spy with my little eye something beginning with Y."

"What?" asked Keith.

"I said, I spy with my little eye something beginning with Y," replied Colin.

"What can you see beginning with Y?" asked Keith,

somewhat confused.

"That's what you have to guess," said Colin. "It's the game."

"I don't understand," said Keith.

"Me neither," said Connor.

"Or me," added Karen.

"It's quite simple," said Colin angrily. "If I was to spy something beginning with C. You lot could guess as many times as you wanted and it could be cars, or clouds, or cones, anything beginning with C really."

The rest of the cones thought for a while.

"Right I get it now," said Karen. "Try again."

Colin coughed and cleared his throat. "I spy with my little eye something beginning with Y."

"Cars?" said Karen.

"No, that doesn't begin with Y."

"Clouds?" said Keith.

"That doesn't begin with Y either," said Colin, getting quite impatient. "Let me explain the rules again."

Colin tried to explain the rules to the very simple game for over two hours. Still none of the others stood at the side of the motorway could see what he meant. He began to get quite cross and started to shout.

"There's no need to shout," said Carla. "We're not deaf."

"No you're not deaf," shouted Colin, whilst pacing up and down in front of the others. "Just stupid."

The other cones gulped, they didn't like being shouted at.

"It's very easy," continued Colin. "I say I can spy something beginning with a letter and you lot have to guess things beginning with that letter."

"Oh, I see. I understand now," said Keith. "Try again."

Colin cleared his throat one more time. "I spy with my little eye something beginning with Y."

"Clouds?" asked Keith.

"No no no!" shouted Colin.

The other cones still hadn't understood the game when darkness fell over the motorway. The workmen had gone home and left the cones where they were so that the cars wouldn't drive on the wet paint and leave white tyre prints across the motorway. The cones were going to be there all night. It was going to be a long night, a long cold night. Frost started to form on the ground and the trees. It sparkled in the headlights of the cars as they rushed past to their destinations.

Finally, two and a half hours after night had come the cones understood the rules to the game.

"Yacht?" asked Keith.

Colin sighed. "Where can you see a yacht?"

"Well I can't, but it does begin with a Y."

"Yak?" asked Carla, excitedly. She felt sure she had the right answer.

"No," Colin sighed again.

They understood the rules, but they didn't understand they had to be able to see the things that began with the letter.

Suddenly Karen shouted. "Why can't I move anymore?"

"That doesn't even begin with Y," Colin groaned and covered his eyes with his hands. "Look it's quite simple..."

"I can't move either," said Keith.

"Nor me," said another cone.

"Me neither," added a fourth.

Colin tried to jump forwards just to prove the others wrong. He couldn't, he was stuck. He tried again. Still he couldn't move. "We're stuck!"

"What are we going to do now?" all the cones asked together.

"I don't know," said Colin. "Am I expected to answer all the questions all of the time?" said Colin.

"Yes," they all replied.

"Well, I suppose we will just have to wait until the workmen come back in the morning and pick us up. Now something else that begins with Y please."

Day broke and the workmen returned to collect all of the cones after their long night. None of the cones had managed to guess what Colin could see beginning with Y. Most of the cones were complaining all night long about the cold and the fact they couldn't move, they all seemed to be stuck fast to the road. The sunlight glistened on the frost covering the fields and the road. It covered the cones too, their orange bits sparkled in the sunlight nearly as much as the white reflective covers did. The workmen sat in the cab of Lawrence and had a cup of tea from their flask and a sandwich each while they all tried to do the crossword in the newspaper.

After about half an hour they had finished their breakfast and two of them climbed out of Lawrence's cab and started to lift the cones from the road and place them in the back of the lorry, whilst the third, the manager, tried to finish the crossword.

The first workman bent down and tried to lift Katie, he

couldn't, she was stuck to the floor. He gave her a kick, but still she didn't move. Two more kicks and a bit of shouting and still Katie sat, stuck to the road.

"I don't know why he was shouting at me," she whispered to Carla. "It's not my fault. I wish I could move. I bet it's lovely and warm in the back of Lawrence."

A second workman tried to lift Katie. He too kicked her a couple of times before giving up. The manager left the cab with his paper tucked under his arm and mumbled some words to the two workmen. They all began shouting at each other and pointing to the cones stuck to the road. After a quick argument, all three men were back in Lawrence's cab driving along the motorway away from the cones.

"Where are they going?" Keith asked.

"I don't know," replied Colin. "Have you seen anything beginning with Y yet?"

An hour or so had past and still no one had guessed Colin's spying.

"Amber lights," shouted Keith.

"How many more times do I have to explain the rules?" snapped Colin. "Amber lights begins with an A. What you should be looking for begins with a Y."

"No. Amber lights coming along the motorway."

The cones looked up the motorway and, sure enough, flashing amber lights were coming along the road.

"What is it?" asked Katie.

"Am I supposed to answer every question?" Colin snapped again.

"It's Grace," shouted Keith.

"Huh," groaned Colin. "That's all we need, her coming over here and laughing at us for being stuck to the road."

"Perhaps she's here to help us," added Carla.

"I doubt it," mumbled Colin.

Grace sped towards the cones, and sprayed them with salty tasting stones. "Ha ha," she laughed. "You cones are so clever, but you need the help of an old gritter to help you move."

As the salty stones landed on the floor around the bases of the cones the ice slowly began to melt.  They were soon able to move a little bit at first and then with a bit of a struggle Colin managed to jump into the air.

"I'm free!" he shouted.

"Not without my help," Grace called, as she thundered past for a second time, spraying them with more salty stones.

It wasn't much longer before all the cones were safely warming themselves in the back of Lawrence and on their way home to the yard close to the M4 motorway.

"What was it that you could spy that began with Y, Colin?" Karen asked.

"Yellow vans."

"But there weren't any yellow vans," Keith protested.

"There would have been if one of the cars passing at the time had broken down."

"That's cheating," the others chorused.

"How would you lot know?" asked Colin, turning his back on the others. "You didn't understand the rules anyway."


If you ever see a gritter trundling up and down the roads spreading grit on a cold and frosty day, remember to give it a wave. It may be gritting the roads to stop all the cars and lorries slipping on the ice. It might be Grace spreading grit to free cones who have been frozen to the road. If you do wave at her she probably won't wave back. She isn't being rude she is just still trying to spy something beginning with Y.

# Beached Cones

Have you ever been to the seaside and seen a traffic cone
lying on the beach covered in seaweed? Did you think that it
had been put there by someone who wanted to build a road on
the sand and forgot about it? Or did you think that the cone had
gone on holiday to the seaside? Maybe cones do go on holiday,
or maybe they don't. Perhaps there is a totally different reason
for a cone being on a beach.

It was late one February night, or perhaps very early one
February morning, on the M4 motorway. It was very foggy, the
fog was so thick the cones stretched out along the first lane of
the motorway could not see each other and they were only
spaced a little way apart. They were calling to each other to
make sure they hadn't been left on the road all on their own.

"Shhhhh!" shouted Colin. "What's that noise?"

The other cones all held their breath and listened hard. There
was the noise of a lorry, a big lorry, thundering towards them. It
sounded like it was going far to fast for the driver to be able to
see in the fog. It was. There was a sudden squeal of brakes and
the cab of the lorry smashed into Sally, the sorry for any delay
sign. Sally flew high into the air and was knocked to the side of
the road by the trailer. The lorry carried on skidding along the

road, smashing into all of the cones stood by the side of the road. Some cones where flattened, some were scattered all over the road and some had been sent flying onto the grass beside the motorway.

When the lorry finally screeched to a halt the bumper was just centimetres from Colin's white reflective cover. The road looked like a battlefield, there were battered and bumped cones lying everywhere groaning in pain. Sally was lying dented in the long, wet grass. Two of the cones, Casper and Clarissa, had been thrown into the fast running stream that ran along the edge of the motorway. They coughed and spluttered as they were dragged along in the muddy water.

By the time the sun came up Casper and Clarissa found themselves bobbing along in a slow running muddy river.

"I'm scared," said Clarissa, as she struggled to stay above the water.

"Don't be silly. This is an adventure, just like the one Keith and Katie had when they ran away."

"I know, but they knew their way back to the yard," moaned Clarissa. "We don't even know where the yard is."

"We know where the yard is, it is near to the M4 motorway," replied Casper. He thought for a moment. "We just don't know where the motorway is, that's all."

Fields of cows and crops went past them as they slowly bobbed along the river. They saw fishermen sat beside the river casting their lines in to catch a fish.

"What are they doing?" asked Clarissa spluttering, because she had just swallowed a lot of muddy water.

"Fishing."

"Do they eat the fish they catch from this dirty water?" asked Clarissa.

"No. When they've caught them they throw them back to catch another day."

"Why?"

"I don't know," answered Casper. "But then again would you want to eat something that lives in this water."

Clarissa looked into the brown water around her, it was so dirty she couldn't see her base. "No."

Suddenly Clarissa stopped bobbing along in the flow of the river, she was still. Casper floated past slowly.

"What are you doing?" he called. "Try to keep up."

"I can't," she replied. "I'm stuck on something."

She was stuck on something, it was a fisherman's line. She started to move backwards up the river.

"Casper help!"

There was nothing Casper could do. Everyone knows cones

can't swim. All he could do was watch as his friend was pulled up stream and he continued to float down the river.

Clarissa was dragged along for quite some time, she was taken under the water a few times and she was coughing and spluttering. She could hear one of the fishermen call to his friend, he said something about bringing a net because he had caught a big one. Clarissa was very confused by this as she wasn't very big at all, in fact she was one of the smaller cones from the yard.

There was a look of disgust on the fisherman's face when Clarissa was finally pulled out of the water. The fishing line was tangled all around the little cone.

"Kids," he moaned, as he took out a knife and cut his line.

"Why do they do things like that? They should leave cones alone at the side of the road, not throw them into rivers."

After cutting Clarissa free he promptly threw her back into the river and she bobbed along following Casper, only now she had fishing line wrapped around her.

When darkness fell Clarissa finally caught up with Casper, he was stuck at the side of the river in a branch from a tree dangling into the dirty water. As Clarissa floated past the line around her entangled Casper too and they both floated freely along the river. She told Casper how pleased she was to be back with him. She also told him what the fisherman had said about her being a "big one."

By daybreak the river had joined another wider, faster flowing river. The water was still muddy but it rushed along past all the scenery. The two cones sped past houses and boats, rushed under bridges, banging into the bricks on the supports as they did so.

They sped along in the new river for two or three more days before the scenery started to change. There were strange birds flying overhead squawking to each other. The boats on the water were bigger and the river was wider now than ever before.

"Where are we going?" asked Clarissa nervously.

"To the seaside," answered Casper excitedly.

Sure enough the river flowed straight into very salty tasting water. (Clarissa knew it was salty because she had swallowed plenty of it.) The two cones bobbed up and down on the waves for several days. Fish nibbled at their bases, it tickled. Great clumps of green seaweed were caught up in the fishing line tied between the two of them.

Finally the waves pushed them closer towards the coast and after almost three weeks of floating they landed on the sandy shore. They lay there tied together on the wet sand surrounded by clumps of seaweed and bits of rubbish, as the small waves lapped against them.

"Where are we?" asked Clarissa.

"Lost," replied Casper very sadly.

Many days went by before a team of school children came onto the beach carrying huge bags. Up until then the only things Casper and Clarissa had seen on the beach was a man walking two big black dogs. The children were picking up all the rubbish that was strewn over the beach, plastic bottles, and bits of wood, even a pair of old trainers. One boy spotted the two cones lying by the water edge and called to his teacher. They came over to where the two cones were. The cones were dirty, smelly and covered in fisherman's line and seaweed. They were picked up and dropped into a large black bag along with all the other bits of rubbish.

The two cones were taken to the school where the children came from and tipped out onto a large piece of plastic which covered the carpet in the classroom, along with many other fishy smelling pieces of rubbish. The children began sorting through the rubbish and putting it all into separate piles.

"What does WCC mean?" one of the children asked the teacher looking on the bottom of the two cones.

"Pardon?"

"WCC, it's written here on the bottom of these cones in big black letters."

"Wiltshire County Council," Casper whispered, "We are going to get home."

Three days later, after the two cones had been cleaned up and stripped of the fishing line and seaweed, a van pulled into the school gates. It was Vera. The cones were loaded aboard and driven back to the yard close to the M4 motorway. They were welcomed back to the yard with cheers from all the other cones. Sally was sat in the shed she had been straightened out but was still feeling a little sore in places. Some of the other cones that were injured in the crash were wrapped in plastic bandages. Colin leapt from the top of the pile to greet them.

"Where have you two been?" he asked. "We were all worried about you."

"To the seaside," replied Casper.

"Wow. What was it like?" asked Keith. "Was it fun?"

"Oh yes," chuckled Clarissa. "More fun than just running away for a few days like you and Katie. We went on holiday."

"Did you get our postcard?" asked Casper.

The whole shed laughed. Then the two cones told stories about their seaside adventure until bedtime.


If ever you see any cones lying on a beach next to the shore, pick them up and have a look on their bases for their letters. The letters will tell you where they belong. They will always want to get home, they are not there for the new road on the sand. They may have been on a holiday. As you probably know, holidays always have to end and you have to go home eventually, no matter how much you enjoyed it.

# One Good Little Cone

Have you ever seen a statue in a town wearing an orange and white cone for a hat?  Did you think that vandals had stolen the cone and placed it there?  Did you think the statue thought it would be funny to look like a witch or a wizard?  Maybe vandals had stolen the cone.  Maybe the statue did want to look funny.  Maybe there is a totally different reason for a statue to wear a cone as a hat.

It was a hot summer day and the cones from the yard close to the M4 were on duty in the town centre, they were lined up along the middle of the road so the workmen could dig up the road for the third time that year and put some more cable under it.  Tommy and Terry the two sets of traffic lights were busy stopping traffic whenever they felt like it at either end of the tunnel of cones.  The workmen were busy digging with very noisy machines, apart from the manager who was asleep in the front seat of Leonard, they were all completely ignoring the cones.

"I wish they would turn those machines off," said Colin to no-one in particular.  "I can't hear myself think,"

"What do you need to think about?" asked Keith.  "All we have to do is stand here getting in the way of all the cars.  Look how much traffic we've already got stuck in queues."

"I know all about the traffic," replied Colin. "Stopping traffic is boring. It's been done before. We need to do something more interesting, something to show the workmen we are something more than things that stand at the side of the road so they can work in safety."

"But that's exactly what we are," said Connie, a small and very well behaved cone.

"Yeah, but I want something more than that," Colin replied. "I want people to laugh whenever they see me. I want to have adventures. I want excitement in my life."

"Well you won't find all that sat at the side of the road," said Keith.

"I know," said Colin.

"So what are you going to do?" asked Keith.

"When the workmen stop for lunch I'm going to make a dash for the hedges in the park and hide until it is dark. Then when it is dark I'm going to find somewhere to be ready for people to laugh at me when they go to work in the morning."

When lunchtime came the workmen all stopped work and went to the café for something to eat. Now was Colin's chance to make a break for freedom, he quickly hopped across the road, when the cars had stopped, and made a dive for the hedge at the

edge of the park. He lay under the hedge panting for his breath
and waited.

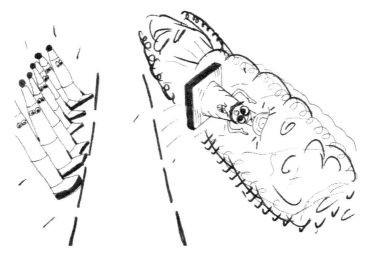

Lying under a hedge for the afternoon isn't very comfortable
and Colin tried to go to sleep to pass the time. He tried to count
cars as they passed. In fact he tried everything he could think of
to pass the time. Nothing worked, he was bored and it still
wasn't dark. He was beginning to think his idea to run away
probably wasn't a good one.

Finally the workmen began packing up their tools for the day
as the sun started to set making the sky turn orange. It wouldn't
be long before Colin could make a run for his new resting place
for the night. He wondered where he would eventually end up,
it had to be somewhere no cone had ever been before and it had
to be somewhere funny, somewhere that would make people's
sides split when they laughed so hard on their way to work.

In the middle of the park Colin saw the place where he would go. It was a statue of a man in old Victorian clothes. He didn't know who the statue was, but that didn't really matter.

When it was totally dark, apart from the glow from the street lights, Colin began making his way across the park towards the old statue. He had to stop every now and then when he thought people might see him moving. Soon he reached the bottom of the statue and started to climb up. It wasn't long before he was perched on top of the top hat the statue was wearing.

Colin's orange light was still flashing in the moonlight. Keith and the other cones could see Colin's flashing light from where they were standing.

"He's done it," said Keith.

"Who's done what?" asked Connie.

"Colin. He's somewhere funny. I hope everyone laughs at him when they see him in the morning."

Everyone did laugh when they saw Colin perched on top of the statue in the park, his light flashing like a lighthouse. People in cars slowed down to look as they drove by, people on buses pressed their faces against the windows to get a better look at the funny cone. All the people who walked through the park on their way to work or school stopped and laughed, no matter how grumpy they looked. Colin was very pleased with himself, he had made even the grumpiest of people laugh on their way to work. There was only one group of people who didn't find Colin's joke funny, that was the workmen when they arrived at the hole in the road. The manager sent one of the men into the park to collect Colin from his perch and return him to his position in the road. When the workman climbed up the statue to collect the naughty cone he was muttering something about naughty children stealing things. Colin had a little chuckle to himself. When he was back in position in the road all of the cones cheered very quietly so the workmen wouldn't hear them.

"Everyone laughed this morning, Colin. Well done," said Keith when Colin stood next to him.

"I know. If they laughed that much at one cone, think how funny all of us will be tomorrow morning."

What a great idea? All of the cones could make their way to a funny place when it was dark and then in the morning everyone would be laughing so much they wouldn't be able to drive their cars, they would be walking all over the road and causing huge traffic jams.

When darkness had fallen and the workmen had gone home all of the cones set about their mission, all of the cones except one. Connie was too well behaved to start messing about and making people laugh, her job was to stop cars falling into the hole in the road and that was the job she was going to do. The rest of the cones ran through the park and around the streets looking for somewhere funny to stand ready for the morning. Some of the cones stood on top of statues, some sat on the swings and roundabouts in the park, some even stood on the roofs and boots of parked cars in a long line like fins on the back of dinosaurs. Everyone who saw the cones in the morning would have to hold their sides together because they would be sure to split with laughter.

Not long after all of the cones had found somewhere funny to stand a little red car drove along the road. It stopped at Tommy's red traffic light at the beginning of where the cones had once stood. The light turned green and the car drove along the road, the driver was moaning about the traffic light stopping traffic for no reason when Connie saw the headlights rushing towards her. The car was going to fall into the hole the cones should have been guarding. She hopped into the middle of the road in the hope that the driver of the little red car would see her and stop before it fell into the hole.

The driver of the car did see Connie and stamped on the brakes, the little red car skidded on the road and smashed into the cone knocking her into the hole. The little red car stopped at the very edge of the hole in the road. The driver got out of the car and phoned the police straight away.

Three police cars arrived at the hole in the road within minutes. Shortly afterwards Lance, Leslie and all of the workmen arrived on the scene. The policemen asked the workmen questions. The workmen rushed around the town looking for all the cones to put them back in the place where they should be. They where muttering under their breath about vandals hiding the cones and how dangerous it could have been, as they rounded up all the other cones. Colin was very cross, none of the workmen found him funny at all, sitting on top of a lamppost, his light still flashing brightly.

Connie lay in the bottom of the hole, dented and dirty.

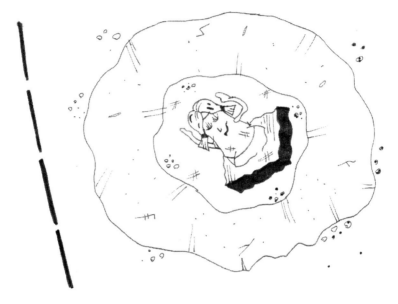

She was pleased she had stopped a nasty accident from happening, but she was also incredibly angry with all of the other cones for leaving her alone. When she and the rest of the cones where stood back in place she told them all off. They all said sorry for what they had done, all except Colin, he was proud of the mayhem they had caused. He only expected to make people laugh not cause a car to skid off the road and nearly fall into a hole. Maybe next time the car would fall into the hole, next time he would make sure all of the cones went with him, all the cones and even the traffic lights. Unfortunately the next time he and the other cones could leave their positions by the hole would be a while because, Leslie and two of the workmen stayed by the road works all night to make sure none of the cones where stolen by any vandals and hidden again.

If you ever do see a traffic cone on top of a statue or a lamppost, please try not to laugh, no matter how funny you think it looks. Vandals may have stolen the cone or it might have tried to find somewhere funny to stand to make people laugh. Either way the cone in the funny place is not doing his or her job properly and may cause an accident. Cars, people or very good little cones like Connie might get hurt. We don't want that to happen do we?

# Ice Cream Cone

Have you every seen orange and white traffic cones in a town centre? Did you think that they were out shopping? Why else would they be there? If it was a town centre that didn't allow cars to drive through, they couldn't be there to stop cars could they? Perhaps they are out shopping, or perhaps they are there for a completely different reason. Maybe we can find out.

It was a scorching hot summer's day, the cones from the depot close to the M4 were on duty on a road not far from the shopping centre, guarding a hole the workmen were digging.

Terry and Tommy, the traffic lights, were stopping traffic whenever they felt like it. Cars waited in the heat to get past the roadworks with their windows wound right down. Colin was hot. Colin was so hot he was feeling a little bit dizzy. His light was flashing very slowly and dimly.

At lunchtime the workmen stopped digging and sat down for a well-deserved break, they had worked very hard that morning. They drank great gulps of fizzy pop straight from the bottle. They wiped the sweat from their foreheads with their sleeves, as they sat on the side of the road eating their lunch.

"I wish I could get a drink to help me cool down," gasped Colin. "I'm so hot."

"Me too," agreed Clyde. "A swim would be better."

"I just wish we could move into the shade," said Katie. "I think my base is melting to the road."

Just then the cones saw the manager of the depot pull up next to them in Vera. He stepped out of the little van and handed each of the three workmen an ice cream in a cone with a chocolate flake pushed deep into it.

"What are they?" asked Clyde, looking at the ice creams.

"I don't know," replied Katie. "But they look like they are helping cool down the workmen."

"They are ice creams," said Colin. "I've seen them before when I was working at a school fete a few years ago. You get them from a van or a shop. They can be all sorts of different colours."

"What do they do?" asked Clyde and Katie together.

"Cool you down," replied Colin.

The three cones soon decided they needed an ice cream. They talked about how they could go and get one. However, none of them knew where the ice cream shop or van was to go and collect one. The only person who would know was Vera, because she had taken the manager there. The three cones devised a plan.

The plan was quite simple. Clyde was the smallest so he could get to the shop where ice creams could be found. Find some ice creams. Get back to Colin and Katie at the side of the road and let them cool down with the ice creams.

Clyde sneaked to the back of Vera and opened her back doors. He leapt on board and asked one of the spare cones to take his place on the side of the road. None of them would as it was very hot work and they liked it in the back of Vera, because it was so cool. Clyde soon lost his temper, he was hot and bothered and all he wanted was an ice cream to cool him down. He pushed Carlos out of the van and onto the road.

"What does he think he's doing?" Carlos protested as Colin and Katie dragged him into place. "I've got a very important job,"

"Getting us some ice cream," replied Colin. "Now shut up and stand still."

Clyde waited in the back of Vera for only a short while before she stopped outside a shop that had lots of pictures of what looked like ice creams in the window. The manager of the depot was going in to buy more ice creams for other workmen around the town.

When no one was looking Clyde climbed out of the back of Vera and hid behind a dustbin. He waited until the coast was clear. Vera and the manager drove off with three more ice creams, Clyde slowly made his way around the back of the shop and waited by a door with peeling brown paint on it.

It was dark before the door was finally opened, while the man was at the big bins putting out the rubbish Clyde nipped inside unnoticed. He hid behind some boxes in the dark storeroom. Clyde had made it, he had got to the shop, all he had to do now was find some ice creams and make his way back to where his friends were waiting for him.

Clyde couldn't see any ice creams, all he could see were hundreds of boxes of cones, shelves full of bottles of strawberry sauce and chocolate sauce and packets of chocolate flakes.

There wasn't any ice cream anywhere to be seen. Where could all the ice creams be?

He waited in his hiding place behind the boxes until the lights went off and he was sure the staff of the shop had gone home before he started to explore.

It was very dark, Clyde could hardly see a thing, he wished he was bigger and had a flashing light on his head like Colin. Unfortunately he didn't and he had to fumble around in the darkness in search of the ice creams.

Eventually he found a sign in the darkness next to a door, it said *Freezer*. Freezers are cold, thought Clyde. Ice creams are cold too. Perhaps the freezer was where the ice creams were?

It wasn't too long before he managed to open the door, there was a hiss as the cold air rushed out and into the warmth of the storeroom. Clyde quickly dashed inside and gazed around the shelves.

"Ice cream!" he whispered to himself. "Loads of it."

He turned himself upside down and leapt from shelf to shelf filling himself up with all sorts of ice cream. There were huge dollops of red, pink, green, yellow and brown ice cream inside him within minutes. His body was filled with a whole rainbow of ice cream colours. He jumped down from the shelf he was on, the whole freezer shook as he landed on the floor. The door slowly started to swing on its hinges. The door was closing.

Clyde rushed towards the closing door. He was too late, the door slammed shut just before he could get to the opening.

There he stood, on his head, full of ice cream in the coldest place he had ever been. He shook and shivered and cursed his bad luck. He wished he was hot at the side of the road again. Eventually he fell asleep leant up against the door.

The shop owner opened the door to the freezer when he came into work in the morning. To his surprise an orange and white traffic cone filled with a mixture of ice creams fell onto the floor by his feet. He had an amazing idea as he looked at the slowly melting ice cream in the cone. He could use the cone to stand outside his shop as an advert.

And that was exactly what he did. He cleaned the ice cream out of Clyde and painted him brown, just like an ice cream cone. Then he filled him up with lots of plastic coloured balls that looked like scoops of ice cream.

Clyde was then placed, upside down, on the pavement outside the shop doorway next to a sign saying, *Mario's Ice Creams. All flavours.*

Back at the side of the road Colin and Katie were getting worried because Clyde hadn't returned. Carlos moaned that he was hot and should still be in the back of Vera in the shade.

"He'll be back soon," said Colin. "He can't be too far away."

"I hope he hasn't got lost," replied Katie. "I'm going to go and look for him." With that she hopped off in search of her friend.

To this day she still hasn't found him, but she won't give up looking until she does. And to this day Clyde still stands all day outside the doorway of the ice cream parlour and at night he is taken inside so vandals don't steal him, so he has never managed to escape, yet.

If you ever see a cone on the pavement in a shopping centre while you are out shopping it might well be just out shopping too, or it could well be Katie still searching for Clyde. If you do see her please point her in the right direction of the nearest ice cream parlour, because she has been looking for him for a long while. Next time you go to an ice cream parlour have a look to see if you can find a cone stood upside down outside advertising ice creams. If you do find one, wait until there are no grown-ups around, go up to it and whisper, "Clyde is that you?" If it is Clyde he will definitely answer you. When he does maybe you could help him get home to the maintenance yard close to the M4 motorway.

# Delaying Cones

Have you ever been a passenger in a car and seen signs at the side of the road saying, sorry for any delay? Have you ever wondered if the signs were really sorry for any delay or if they were just saying it to make drivers feel better? Perhaps they really are sorry, but maybe there is a completely different reason why they stand in the road next to loads of cones.

All of the cones from the yard close to the M4 were inside the shed piled up out of the rain. The weather had not been very good recently so they hadn't had much work to do. Colin was marching up and down in front of the piles of orange and white cones trying to think up a new idea for some sort of fun.

"I'm bored," he said. "What we need is to block off the motorway again, like we did before. We need to cause some long traffic jams."

"Why?" asked Connie.

"Because that's our job."

"I thought our job was to warn people about dangers on the roads and stop cars falling into the holes the workmen have dug," said Connie.

"Have you not read what it says on the front of Sally, Scott, Suzie and Simon, the signs?" asked Colin.

"Yes."

"And what does it say?"

Connie looked at Colin and replied. "Sorry for any delay."

"Exactly. Sorry for any delay," shouted Colin. "People expect delay, and for that we are sorry. If we don't cause traffic jams there won't be any delay, and if there isn't any delay, we don't have to be sorry about it. If we don't have to be sorry for not causing any delay then the four signs won't have a job. And do you know what they do to signs that don't have a job?"

"No," answered Connie a little worried now.

"They get sent to a scrap metal plant and after being crushed and beaten they are cut up and made into tins. Tins that hold cat food." He paused to let the speech sink into the ears of all the cones. "Is that what you want? Do you want our friends the signs turned into cat food tins?"

The four signs shuffled round in their stack to look at Connie, a once heroic cone even if she was only small. Connie looked back at the signs, they were her friends, and they helped to warn people of the dangers in the roads too.

"No," she slowly replied.

"So what we need to do," began Colin, as he marched up and down in front of the cones, puffing his chest out. "Is cause some traffic jams to stop our good friends, the signs, being turned into cat food tins."

"Or dog food tins," said Conor.

"What?" asked Colin.

"Well they could be made into dog food tins. Or, in fact, any type of tin for holding any kind of food for any animal really."

"Conor?"

"Yes Colin?"

"Shut up."

"Sorry, Colin."

The cones sat up long into the night planning what they could do to stop the four signs being turned into cat food tins or, any type of tin for holding any type of food for any animal really. Colin remained in charge of the meeting, he paced up and down giving orders to the others, and he told them when they could speak and he decided if their ideas were good or if they were totally useless. This was Colin's meeting and he was in charge.

"Why don't we stand on top of statues' heads again?" asked Clive.

"Been done before," replied Colin.

"How about a road block?" asked Kevin.

"Boring."

"What about a crash involving a lorry carrying lots and lots of cones? It would take ages to clear us all up and then we would cause a huge traffic jam," said Connie.

"That's brilliant," replied Colin. "I thought you didn't like the idea of stopping cars just for the sake of it."

"I hate the idea of my friends being made into cat food tins more," answered the little cone.

"Or indeed any type of tin, for any kind of food, for any animal really."

"Shut up, Conor!" all the cones chorused together.

It was still dark, the sun hadn't climbed out of bed yet, but the idea was put into motion. All of the cones along with the four signs, climbed into the back of Lance. It was much easier to escape from the yard this time as Grace was away having her brakes repaired, so she was unable to try and stop them. Lance charged up to the gates and smashed through them, they swung open so hard they fell off their hinges.

"Which road do you want me to crash on?" Lance asked Colin.

"Any one you like. Just don't do it on the motorway."

"Why not?"

"Motorways have got three lanes on both sides of the road so it will be easier to get around us. What we need is a busy road that only has one lane on either side then we can cause really long traffic jams."

"I know just the place," said Lance. He chuckled to himself as he trundled along the road.

After a fairly short drive the lorry with it's very naughty load was at the bottom of two hills in a valley, on a road with high hedges on either side, there was no way around the road on the grass areas.

"Will this do?" asked Lance hopefully.

"This is just perfect," replied an excited Colin.

"Is crashing going to hurt?" asked the lorry.

"No you're not really going to crash, we are just going to make it look like you crashed by tipping you over onto your side."

Lance parked himself across the road blocking both lanes and the cones all jumped out and stood on one side of him. Then they all, (apart from Colin, who was in charge and couldn't possibly push,) pushed the big lorry until he tipped onto his side.

"Perfect," shouted Colin. "Now all of you scatter yourselves over the road and in the hedges and make it look like you have just fallen out of Lance."

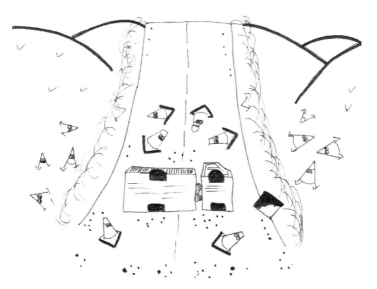

Colin watched everyone take up their positions and moved some of them around until they were in a better place. "Just perfect," he said when all the work was done.

Even the four signs had managed to look as if they had fallen out of the lorry, they laid on the ground, sign side up so anyone passing would see the message, because they really were sorry for any delay, they just wanted to keep their jobs.

As the sun started to rise over the hills the traffic started to build up on the road. People in their cars were trying to get to work on time. There were lots of red faces on the people as they joined the long queues. Most of the people got out of their cars and after a brief speech on their mobile phones, they began picking up the cones and stacking them at the side of the road.

It wasn't long before the police and fire brigade turned up at the scene. The policemen helped to pick up the cones and tried to calm down some of the more angry drivers. The fire brigade used a crane to get Lance back onto his wheels then they, along with a lot of people from the cars, pushed him to the side of the road out of the way. The good thing was, he still blocked one of the lanes. The traffic had to be directed by the policemen until the manager of the yard and his workmen came and collected all the cones and placed them in the back of Lance ready for the drive home. The last thing to go into the back of Lance was Sally. One of the drivers from the cars saw the sign and wound down his window and shouted at the workmen.

"Sorry for any delay! Sorry for any delay!" He shook his fist at them too. "I'm so late this has cost me a lot of money. I ought to make mince meat out of you lot."

Then the workmen placed Sally into the back of Lance and drove him away to unblock the road.

"Mince meat could be stored in tins too," said Conor.

"SHUTUPCONOR!!!" all the cones shouted together.

"Colin."

"Yes, Connie?"

"Will the signs be safe now?"

"I hope so, but only for a month or two."

"What will happen then?" asked the little cone.

"We will have to do something else."

"Good," said Connie with a big smile on her face. "That was fun."

If you ever see lots of cones lying across the road, don't be angry that they have slowed you down. Have a look to see if there are any signs there too. If there are give them a wave because they are only trying to keep their jobs, and stop themselves being made into cat food tins.

"Or any type of tin, for any type of food."

"Shut up, Conor!"

# Football Cones

Have you ever seen cones stood on the ground in a park? Did you think they were there to feed the ducks? Maybe you thought they wanted to play on the swings and the slides? Did you think they had been placed there so people could use them as goalposts when they played football? Perhaps they were being used as goalposts. Perhaps there was a completely different reason.

Colin and the rest of the cones were working on the road next to the park in the town centre. Darren the digger was digging a deep hole, Vera was there too as she had brought the workmen and the cones to the road. The workmen were using all kinds of digging equipment, the whole place was very noisy.

The cones were bored, as always. They were fed up with having to stand at the side of the road and just watch the world passing by, while it was too noisy to talk to each other.

"I wish they would stop being so noisy," shouted Colin.

"What?" asked Clara.

"I said, I wish they would stop being so noisy," Colin shouted again.

"I can't hear you, the workmen are being far too noisy," Clara called.

"That's what I just said."

"What?"

"It doesn't matter," Colin shouted at the top of his plastic lungs.

"Pardon?" shouted Clara.

"SHUTUP!"

"I wish they would," Clara screamed. "It's far to noisy here."

Across the road there were some boys playing football in the park, they had their jumpers lying on the floor to mark the goal posts.

Colin wished he was a jumper, he would much rather sit in the park watching boys play football than stand in the road next to all the noisy machines. He had an idea, an idea that would need Vera's help. He slowly moved close enough to Vera so she could hear him when he whispered his plan to her. None of the workmen noticed him moving, as they were all very busy with their noisy machines. Vera couldn't hear Colin whispering so he had to shout. It didn't matter that he was being so loud because the men and their machines were being far too noisy to hear his voice. As soon as Vera had heard Colin's plan she leapt into action. She had always wanted to be naughty just like the cones but never got asked to do anything bad. Vera slowly let her handbrake off and began, creeping at first, down the hill of the road.

Soon she was trundling towards the bottom of the hill and careering into all of the other cones guarding the hole. The workmen hurriedly stopped what they were doing and threw their tools onto the ground so they could chase after the naughty, runaway van. The three workmen ran as fast as they could to try and catch up with Vera. The first workman was a bit too fat to be running after runaway vans and had to sit down at the side of the road until he got his breath back, he mopped his brow with his red and white spotted handkerchief. The other two, younger and fitter workmen, were gaining on the van as it hurtled towards the town centre and the red traffic lights at the bottom of the hill.

"Turn yourselves green!" shouted Vera to the traffic lights. "I'm coming through."

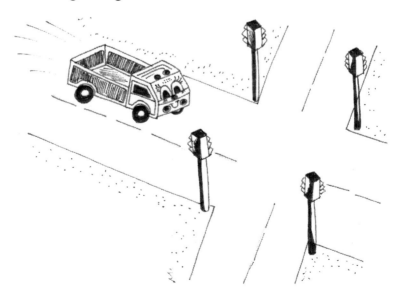

The lights did as they were told and turned themselves green, stopping the traffic coming in the other direction. After all Vera didn't want to cause an accident, all she wanted to do was cause a diversion so her friend could go and watch the football. The two workmen still continued to run after the runaway van. One of them fell over and banged his knee on the kerb at the side of the road. Vera thought she heard him shout something very naughty indeed as he hit the ground, but she wasn't sure. The third workman put his head down and sprinted after Vera, he eventually caught up with her and opened her door. He dived inside, his foot narrowly missing a lamppost as it flashed past the speeding van. He reached out and with all his strength he managed to pull on the handbrake making Vera screech to a halt at the bottom of the hill, just centimetres from a large shop window displaying ladies clothes.

Meanwhile back at the hole in the road Colin seized his opportunity and began hopping towards the park. Clara wanted to watch the football too, so she hopped after the big cone. The two cones dodged traffic and dashed across the road and through the gates of the park.

"Where are the footballers?" asked Clara, looking across the park.

"I don't know," answered Colin. "If you shut up we might be

able to hear them."

The two cones sat in the middle of the park and listened to all the noises around them. They could hear the sound of the traffic driving down the road and they could hear the beeping of horns in the distance near to where Vera had gone. They were probably the beeping horns of people's cars who wanted the van to move out of their way. In the distance they could also hear the sounds of boys shouting to each other. There were words like, "Pass it here," and "GOAL!"

"Over there. That's where the football is." Colin pointed to a bush.

"You can't play football in a bush, the branches will get in the way of the goals," said Clara.

"Not in the bush, you stupid little cone, behind the bush. Can't you hear them?"

"Yes, but I want to see them. I want to join in," replied Clara, kicking an imaginary ball with her base and then trying to head it with her top.

"Well follow me then," said Colin.

Colin hopped off around the bush, Clara followed close behind. When they got to the other side of the bush they saw twenty boys all chasing each other and kicking a ball around the park. All of the boys were covered in mud from their heads to their trainers.

The two cones stood near to the bush watching the boys run around. They stood there for quite some time before one of the boys spotted them and charged towards them. He picked them up and took them over to the football pitch.

"These will be better posts than jumpers," he called to his friends.

He placed the two cones down where one of the sets of jumpers had been and then hung all of the jumpers on top of them so the clothing wouldn't get dirty. Colin moaned under the jumper, all he wanted to do was watch a game of football and all he could see was the inside of a boy's sweaty jumper.

The two cones sat in the darkness of the jumpers for hours listening to the boys score goals and run around. Colin tried to shake the jumpers off his head so he could see what the boys were doing. Every time it looked as if the jumpers were going

to fall off the boy who was in goal came over and put them back
on him so they wouldn't lie on the muddy ground.

The boys finally stopped playing just as the streetlights
started to come on. The work in the road had finished too and
the workmen began packing away all the tools and cones. They
placed all the cones in the back of Vera, who was now parked
with bricks under her wheels so she wouldn't roll away again.

"There's two missing," said one of the workmen.

"So?" said another.

"We've got to take them all back. The manager is
complaining that too many cones have got lost or been found in
strange places recently."

"They are over there in the park," said the third pointing to
the two cones on the grass. "I'll go and get them."

When all of the cones were safely in the back of Vera and on their way home back to the yard close to the M4 motorway Colin began telling them all about the game of football he had seen. Clara said she hadn't seen any of the game because she had had her head covered by a jumper for the whole time. Colin told them everything he had seen. It didn't matter he hadn't seen any of the game, he just told stories of what he thought was going on outside of the jumpers.

"We could have a game ourselves tonight in the yard," said Colin, his light flashed excitedly.

"How?" asked Chris, a very old and tatty cone.

"All we need is a ball of some kind."

"And what are we going to use for goal posts?" Chris asked again.

"You and your three brothers," replied Colin. "You are all too old to run around anyway."

"What about a ball?" asked Clara.

"We can use an old paint tin," answered Colin. "It won't be exactly the same as football, but it will be a start."

That night, when the workmen had dropped all the cones off back at the yard, they had a game of football. Colin's team won, of course, because he was the only cone who knew the rules, or at least that was what he said when any of the other cones thought he was making the rules up just so he could win. They had played all night and only stopped when they saw the sun begin to rise in the sky, as they knew the workmen would be there soon to start their day.

"We won. Another game tonight?" asked Colin, putting away the battered paint tin.

"Yeah, but we'll need a ball," replied Clara.

"We'll have to see if we can find one today."

If you ever see a pair of cones in a park being used as football goal posts, they may have been placed there by some boys to help with their game, or they may just want to watch the game. And if you ever use cones as goal posts please don't put your jumpers over them. If you do they can't watch the game and learn the rules, and cones need to learn the rules so they can beat Colin's team next time. If they don't learn the rules then Colin will keep cheating, and keep winning.

# Party Cones

Have you ever seen orange and white traffic cones being worn as witches' hats by people? Have you seen people shouting through a cone to make themselves heard better? Did you think cones enjoyed being worn as a hat or used as a megaphone instead of being bored at the side of the road? Perhaps sometimes they do, but then again, sometimes they might prefer to be bored along with all of their friends.

All of the cones from the yard close to the M4 were busy working by a hole in the town centre. It was cold, it was the beginning of winter. In fact it was the beginning of December and the start of all the Christmas parties. The hole in the road was going to be there for quite some time and Colin and his friends were going to have to guard it through the days and nights. Once the workmen had finished for the day the cones were left alone.

"Are we going to have some fun tonight?" asked Kyle, a young cone who had never been involved in any of the fun before.

"No not tonight," answered Connie. "Tonight we do as we are supposed to do and guard this hole."

"Why can't we have some fun?" Kyle asked the older and

wiser cone. "This is so boring, just standing here in the middle of the road. There are no cars to stop, and that means there are no angry drivers for us to laugh at."

"Tonight we do as we are told and guard the hole," said Connie.

"Why?"

"Because holes are dangerous and we all learnt our lesson a while back when a car nearly fell into a hole we were supposed to be guarding." Her chest puffed out with pride. "If it wasn't for the courage and bravery of one cone then disaster would have struck and the car or its driver could have been badly injured."

"I heard about that night," began Kyle. "Everyone was having fun and there was this one boring cone who spoiled it. A car falling in a hole would have been so funny."

Connie sighed. She was cross about the way young cones today only wanted to mess about all the time and put their friends or people in danger. "You don't know what you are talking about. Now, just stand there and guard this hole, and if you could do that quietly, in fact, silently it would be great. All right?"

Kyle did not answer.

"Did you hear what I said?" asked Connie angrily.

Still no reply.

"Kyle, answer me.  Did you hear what I said?"

"Yes," replied the young cone in a low whisper.  "But you said I had to be silent so I didn't want to speak."

Connie sighed once again.


Daylight quickly changed into darkness and the flashing lights on top of Colin and some of the other larger cones lit up the rest of the cones.  Kyle was still bored, he began playing I spy with himself, silently of course, as he didn't want to upset Connie.

"I spy with my little eye something beginning with the letter D," he said silently in his head.

"Dark," he quickly replied.

He soon realised a game of I spy is only fun when other cones guess the words and not the cone who thought of the word.  He sighed a long, very bored sigh.

There was soon the sound of people walking along the road.  Kyle wondered if any of them would want to have some fun.  If he hopped onto the pavement and stood right in the middle, if they didn't see him they would fall over him.  That would be so much fun, he thought and chuckled to himself, silently, so he didn't wake up Connie.  He hopped from his place by the hole and onto the pavement.

The three men walking along the pavement did see the little

cone in their way and didn't fall over him. Kyle was a little upset when they walked around him and didn't all fall over in a big heap. He sighed a long bored sigh again.

"I'm never going to have any fun tonight," he said to himself. "I'm bored."

He soon fell asleep in the middle of the pavement and dreamt of having fun with all the other cones doing all the things he had heard them talk about, from stopping cars on the motorway, to running away and seeing the countryside.

He was quickly woken from his dreams when a man, who had been walking along the pavement, spotted him and picked him up from the floor. The man wedged Kyle onto his head and called to his friends, "Look at me," he shouted. "I'm a witch!" He started to do a funny dance, as if he was dancing around a cauldron.

The rest of the man's friends laughed at the joke and kept on walking along the road.

"I'm going to be a witch all night," the man called to his friends, as he ran after them, trying to catch up. "I'll be Wanda, the drunk witch."

"You won't be allowed in the pub with that on your head," answered a lady who was in the group.

"Bet I do," he called back, dancing down the road singing songs about eyes of newt and legs of frog.

"I'm going to a pub," Kyle thought to himself, as he wobbled about on the man's head. "I'm actually going to a pub. None of the cones have ever done that."

The pub the group went to was very busy and full of people celebrating the Christmas period. There was loud music playing, people were dancing and singing. Kyle banged his head on the doorway and fell to the ground when the man he was sitting on didn't duck down quite far enough for him to get through the door.

"Whoops," said the man, picking up Kyle and sticking him back on his head. "I can't be a witch without a hat can I?"

Kyle spent the next half an hour or so sitting on the man's head while he danced and drunk beer. Kyle was enjoying himself so much, even though he occasionally got knocked off the man's head when he banged into a light or a doorway.

Finally Kyle fell off the man's head when he went to the bar to buy some drinks. The man picked the cone up and placed him on his head once again.

"You can't wear that in here, mate," said the barman to Kyle's man.

"But I'm a witch."

"I don't care, you can't wear that in here, mate," the barman said again.

Kyle spent the rest of the evening sat under a table listening to the music that was playing and staring at the legs of the people sat around it. Kyle was bored again. He was just as bored as he was when he was stood by the side of the road.

"I spy with my little eye something beginning with L," he said to himself.

"Legs," he replied. I spy was still just as boring as it was before.

When one of the man's friends went to the bar, Kyle's man decided he wanted some crisps to go with his beer. His friend didn't hear him shout.

"Cheese and onion please," he called.

"What?" asked his friend, holding his hand up to his ear so he could hear better.

"Cheese and onion please," he called again.

"I can't hear you."

With all the loud music playing there was no way the friend at the bar could hear him, he didn't want to get up so he had an idea. He reached under the table and picked Kyle up by his top and then held Kyle's top next to his mouth. At the top of his voice he shouted through the cone. "Cheese and onion please!"

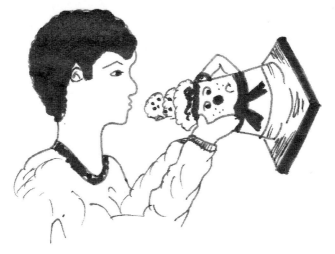

The friend at the bar put his thumbs up to show that he had heard. Kyle's man then placed him back under the table. Kyle's ears were ringing with the sound of the man's voice going right through him. He was fed up, bored and now his ears hurt. He realised that things were only fun when cones invented them and didn't let people get involved, because people were stupid and boring.

Eventually when the pub closed the man placed Kyle on his

head again to be a witch for the long walk home. Every now and then he would shout through Kyle to his friends. All Kyle wanted to do was go to sleep, his head was pounding now after all the shouting through him. He kept wobbling about on the man's head and fell off several times, banging his own head on the pavement. Kyle was very grumpy.

Finally, after the man had been to a kebab shop, Kyle was placed down on the pavement next to the hole where all his friends were. The man stuffed the wrapper of his kebab into the hole on top of Kyle. Sauce and juice dripped down the outside of the little cone leaving red streaks on his bright orange plastic, he was even grumpier than before. Kyle hopped silently back into place beside Connie next to the hole and fell asleep.

The sun rose and lit up all the frost on the ground. The cones were woken up with the bright light and stretched to get rid of the sleep from their plastic bodies. Connie looked at Kyle, he still had red streaks down his body and the kebab wrapper was still stuffed firmly in his head.

"What happened to you?" she asked the dirty looking cone.

"I went to a party," he replied grumpily.

"Was it good?" she asked.

"Not really. The man I was with had far more fun than I did. Things would have been a lot better if all of us had gone instead of me on my own."

"Will you be doing as you are told in the future then?" asked Connie. "Sometimes older cones really are wiser."

"I suppose so," answered Kyle very quietly.

If you ever want to wear a traffic cone as a witch's hat for fun or at a party, don't just pick it up and wear it. If you ask the cone before you put it on your head he will tell you if he wants to come with you to a party or if he would rather stay with his friends. If he does want to come with you and you do take him don't leave him under a table all night, as he will be just as bored there as he was before you took him. And please remember, never ever shout through a cone so people can hear you better, because it gives them a headache and that just makes them grumpy.

# Penguin Cones

Have you ever been on holiday to a far away place that you have to fly on an aeroplane to get to? Have you seen orange and white cones in the airport? Perhaps you might have seen them at the beach? Did you think workmen were working at the airport or the beach and needed the cones to warn people of the danger? Maybe workmen did take them there to warn people of dangers, or perhaps there is a totally different reason.

"This is great fun," said Colin, as a large aeroplane taxied past him.

The cones were working at the local airport guarding a hole in the taxiway the workmen were digging. They had to stand on the taxiway and stop aeroplanes from falling into the hole, because planes were very expensive and falling into a hole would cause a lot of damage to one.

All day the cones watched the aeroplanes taxi past. There were fast, pointy, noisy aeroplanes. Fat, big, slow aeroplanes with propellers on their wings, big, jet aeroplanes with huge wheels as big as humans and lots of people on board, who looked out of the window at the cones as the aeroplane went past. There were even funny looking helicopters with their huge propellers on their heads, and there was one tiny, little aeroplane that was only big enough to carry one pilot and one passenger, both of the people on board waved as they went past the group of cones on the taxiway.

The cones watched all of the aircraft take off along the long road called "the runway," by the workmen. It was a very noisy, but exciting place to be.

"I want to go and see all of the aeroplanes and talk to them," said Cecil, a very old and faded orange cone.

"Don't be so stupid," said Colin. "Aeroplanes can't talk, they are stupid just like cars and need people to drive them."

"I don't care. I want to try and talk to them, they look interesting and they get to go to places far away from holes and workmen."

"Can I come too?" asked Keira, a young and bright orange cone.

"I don't see why not," said Cecil. "We'll go tonight when the workmen have left us."

When darkness arrived and the workmen had gone home the blue lights came on to light up the edges of the taxiway. Cecil and Keira ran off to the big aeroplane park, where all the aeroplanes went to sleep. They wanted to see if they could talk to them and hear stories of far away places. The two cones hopped along the taxiway, following the blue lights and went onto the aeroplane park near to the big buildings with all the lights on. The airport was very busy with trucks and vans driving all over the place. There were even trucks that towed three or four trailers behind them which were full of bags and suitcases, they looked like trains.

Cecil stood by the front wheel of one the biggest aeroplanes on the plane park, he knew that big meant clever. Colin was the biggest of the cones and he was also the cleverest.

"Good evening. I'm Cecil, how are you?" he said.

The aeroplane did not answer.

"Have you been anywhere nice today?"

Still the aeroplane didn't answer.

"Perhaps Colin was right," said Keira to her friend. "Planes are stupid,"

"Colin isn't always right," replied Cecil "This one must be sleeping, we'll try another one."

Throughout the whole night Cecil tried to speak to all of the aeroplanes on the aeroplane park, even the funny looking helicopters and the tiny aeroplane that only held two people.

None of the aeroplanes answered any of his questions.

"Humph! Colin was right, planes are stupid."

The two cones had been trying to talk to the aeroplanes all night and hadn't realised the sun was starting to rise in the sky. They were far too far away from the hole on the taxiway to be able to get back without being seen. They needed to hide, they needed to find somewhere to go and not be seen for the whole day. There was a sign on the side of one of the big buildings, it said "Cargo."

"That must a house for the airport cones," said Cecil, pointing at the building.

"Why?"

"Because Cargo is a cone's name," said Cecil. "I used to work with him years ago until he mysteriously went missing one night when it was windy. I bet he lives there now."

They were both very disappointed not to see piles and piles of cones all around the inside of the building. The building was full of bags and boxes, crates and cages of all shapes and sizes. There were lots and lots of trailers from the van-trains full to the top with bags and suitcases. People were in there too, they were all busy loading things onto the trailers and driving the vans around the huge building, it was a very noisy place.

"Where do we hide?" asked Keira.

There was no time to think, a van-train was thundering towards them loaded with bags.

"Jump!" shouted Cecil.

The pair of cones jumped into one of the trailers as it roared past and hid beneath all of the bags and suitcases.

Cecil tried to talk to the bags to see if they knew where they were going. He soon found out that bags and suitcases were just as stupid as aeroplanes and couldn't talk either.

The van-train stopped at the side of the big aeroplane Cecil had tried to speak to the night before and workmen started to load all of the bags into the back of it. The workmen at the airport were just the same as the workmen by the roads, they all moaned and groaned about how much work they had to do and how short their breaks for tea seemed to be.

"What are these?" asked one of the workmen when he spotted the two cones on the trailer.

"They look like traffic cones," replied another.

"Are they supposed to go on the plane?" asked the first.

"I suppose so."

The two men argued for a while about why anyone would want to take cones as luggage, until a third workman pointed out that when they had loaded the plane they could go and get a cup of tea.

So that was that, Cecil and Keira were on the back of an aeroplane amongst all the bags and suitcase. They were moving in a noisy aeroplane, they were moving very fast. They felt the aeroplane lift off the ground. The cones were flying. They were going somewhere interesting far away from holes in the road.

The journey was very long and tiring and both cones fell asleep soon after the aeroplane took off. They woke up with a start when they heard the screech of wheels on the tarmac of a new runway.

"Where are we?" asked Keira.

"I don't know but it's going to be an adventure," replied Cecil.

The cones and all the bags were unloaded from the aeroplane and put onto trailers from new van-trains. It was very cold and windy. The workmen at the new airport moaned almost as much as the ones Cecil and Keira had left behind. The van-train took all of the baggage to a building and it was all loaded onto a moving floor that went round and round inside the building. There were lots of people waiting by the moving floor inside the building and they picked up the bags and suitcases. Cecil and Keira didn't have a label on them like all the rest of the objects in the back of the aeroplane so no one picked them up from the moving floor.

When all of the people had left the two cones were still going round and round on the moving floor in the building. Eventually the floor stopped moving and one of the moaning workmen came into the room and took the two cones outside and placed them on the cold wet concrete in front of the building.

"What do we do now?" asked Keira. She was quite scared of her new surroundings.

"We wait until it gets dark and no-one is about then we go and explore."

There was a huge sign on the front of the building they were stood by, it said, "Welcome to the Falkland Islands."

"Where are the Falkland Islands?" asked Keira.

"I don't know," replied Cecil. "It's probably where they make forks."

"Oh. Is there a Spoonland Islands and a Knifeland Islands too?"

Cecil thought for a short while and then not wanting to look silly said, "Of course there is."


When night fell the two cones went to explore, they knew there was no point trying to talk to the aeroplanes on the aeroplane park, as they were stupid. They hopped out of the airport and through the gates. They were free to go anywhere. After hopping along a road for a long time they came to a sandy, cold place.

"Where are we now?" asked Keira.

"I think it's called a beach," answered Cecil. "I remember

Casper talking about the one he and Clarissa visited. It sounded just the same as this."

They were both tired after their long flight and the long hop to the beach so they found a sand dune to shelter them from the wind and fell asleep.

When the sun came up the following morning it was still cold and strange little black and white cones that waddled around instead of hopping surrounded the two orange and white cones.

"Good morning," said Cecil. "Are you all traffic cones working to guard a hole in a road?"

"No," answered one of the black and white cones.

"There aren't any roads here on the beach," replied another, as he swallowed a fish whole.

"Then why are you here?" asked Keira.

"We live here," answered a third black and white cone. "This is our home,"

"You live in this sandy place? Why don't you live in a shed like all cones do?" asked Keira, still very surprised to see black and white cones eating fish.

"Because we are penguins," answered the first black and white cone.

"What's a penguin?" asked Cecil.

"We are birds that live on this beach in the Falkland Islands."

"Oh," said Cecil. "Do you make forks then?"

All of the penguins laughed at the silly cone. They thought their visitors were the silliest things they had ever seen.

"What do you do then?" asked Cecil, quite angry about the penguin-cones laughing at him. He was much older and wiser than they were.

"We catch fish in the sea and run around on the beach when the people come so they can take photos of us."

"Great. Can we join in?" asked Cecil.

"I don't see why not. Here's your chance, there are some people coming now."

Sure enough there were three people walking along the beach, they were all holding cameras. The penguin-cones picked up the orange and white traffic cones and ran along the beach with them.

Click, click, went the cameras of the people on the beach. The penguin-cones dived into the sea, still holding the orange and white cones.

"If you see a fish grab it," said one of them.

"Why?" asked Keira and Cecil together.

"Because we are hungry," answered another of the penguin-cones.

"This is so much more fun than standing at the side of a road in England. I want to stay here forever," shouted Keira, as she was lifted out of the water by one of the penguin-cones.

"Me too," replied Cecil. "And it's good that you don't want to go home."

"Why?"

"Because I don't know the way."


If you ever go abroad on holiday and you see orange and white traffic cones on the beach or in the airport say hello to them. They might be working at the airport or they might be on holiday too. Or they might be living there with the rest of the animals on the beach and having lots of fun. If you want to take them back home to England with you and back to the yard close to the M4 ask them first if they want to go, they may want to stay and have more fun. Cecil and Keira have got quite used to eating fish.  They are excellent at catching them, they are much better than the penguins now.

# Racing Cones

Have you ever seen orange and white traffic cones lying squashed on the grass in the middle of a motorway, when all the rest of the cones stood by the side?  Did you think that the wind had carried them onto the busy road?  Or did you think a car had bumped into them and knocked them there?  Perhaps the wind did blow them, or maybe there is a totally different reason for them being there.

It was a quiet Sunday afternoon in the yard close to the M4 motorway.  Colin and the rest of the cones were enjoying a game of football when they heard a vehicle arrive at the padlocked gates.  The gates were unlocked and all of the cones quickly made their way back to the shed to hide and stack themselves on top of one and other.

The vehicle was a lorry, it pulled up next to the shed where Colin and his friends lived.  Two workmen got out of the cab and began removing orange and white cones from the back of the lorry and stacking them in the shed.  There were now hundreds of new cones in the shed stacked in lots of new piles.  The lorry was parked outside the shed next to Lance, Leonard and Leslie the M4 yard's own lorries and the workmen left, locking the gates behind them.

Colin jumped down from the top of the stack he was on and made his way over to the new stacks lining the walls of the shed, the orange light on his head flashing angrily.

"Who are you lot?" he asked quite bluntly. "And what are you doing here in my shed?"

There was some movement in the new stacks and a large cone, just as big as Colin was, with a flashing light on his head moved to the front.

"We," the new cone began. "Are from a yard close to the A316."

"What are you doing here?" snapped Colin. "This is a motorway yard, not a stupid little A-road yard." He was very angry that cones from an A-road were sharing the same shed as his motorway cones.

"Our yard has been closed and we have come here to work with you," answered the new cone.

Colin folded his arms across his chest. "Well, we don't want your sort around here."

"And what exactly is our sort?" asked another of the new cones, jumping down from the top of one of the new stacks.

"Not motorway cones," spat Colin, with venom in his voice.

"So you think you motorway cones are better than us, do you?" the second new cone asked. "I'm sure Kurt and the rest of us are much better than any of you lot."

"A-road cones are not any better than any of us motorway cones. We are the bravest, strongest and cleverest cones there is."

"Yeah?" said Kurt.

"Yeah," snarled Colin.

"Really?" said Kurt.

"Really, really," growled Colin, curling his top lip up to look more menacing.

Both of the cones with flashing lights on their heads stood opposite each other and, if they could, they would have flexed their muscles to make themselves look bigger.

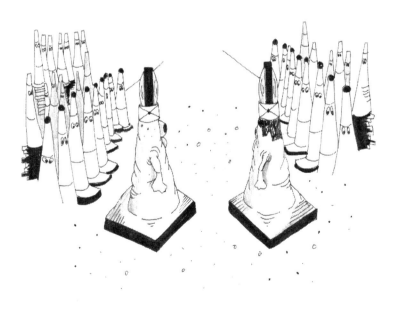

"My cones aren't scared of you lot," snarled Colin. "Are

we?" he shouted to the rest of the motorway cones.

"No!" the motorway cones chorused from their stacks.

"Well, we aren't scared of you lot either," Kurt said. "And we are here to stay. We work harder than any of your cones could ever do. We are better than any cone from a run down motorway yard."

Kurt's cones all cheered when they heard his argument.

It didn't take long before all of the cones, new and old, had jumped down from their stacks and were pushing and shoving each other. They started to fight and the noise of all the cones in the shed arguing was deafening. The fight lasted all through the night. The cones were still fighting when the yard manager unlocked the gates in the morning. The noise of the rusty gates squeaking on their hinges made the cones stop in mid battle. There was no time to hurry back to their stacks in the shed, the cones just had to stay still and wait for the workmen to spot them.

The manager and four workmen saw the cones scattered all over the yard and hastily started to pick them up and return them to their stack in the shed. They moaned about kids breaking into the yard and causing all of the mess. All of the cones were stacked back in the shed, new cones were on top of old ones, and old cones were next to new ones. Both new and old cones were jumbled up and mixed together for the first time.

Some of the cones were needed for a job on the motorway. Four stacks of cones were loaded into the back of Leslie and driven to the hard shoulder on the M4 motorway. Both Colin and Kurt were in the back of the lorry in different stacks.

The workmen unloaded the cones and lined them all up along the white line of the hard shoulder. There were new cones stood next to old cones and old ones stood next to new. Both new and old cones sulked and would not talk to another cone from a different yard.

When the workmen had finished their work for the day the cones were left to line the motorway overnight.

"Now we can see who is the strongest, bravest, cleverest cone," said Colin to Kurt, who was stood next to him.

"How?"

"A competition."

"What happens to the looser?" asked Kurt.

"The looser looses," answered Colin quickly. "The winner will be the leader of all the cones, new and old. He will decide what happens to them all."

"Fine," said Kurt. "What's the competition?"

"A race," replied Colin.

"But where are we going to race to?" asked Kurt, his orange light flashing nervously.

"To the other side of the motorway and back," replied Colin.

"But that's dangerous," moaned Kurt.

"Not if you are brave enough," said Colin, puffing out his plastic chest with pride. "If you were clever enough you would be able to cross the road safely. If you were strong enough you would be able to move quickly."

The race was set. The two cones had to race to the barrier in the middle of the motorway and back to the hard shoulder. The first one to reach the hard shoulder would be the winner and would become the leader of all the cones. They stood at the side of the road and waited for the race to start.

Connie was to start the race, "Three, two, one, go!" she shouted.

The road was very busy, but Kurt started to move forwards. He quickly hopped to across the first lane, then hopped across the second lane and finally dived for the barrier just narrowly missing the front bumper of a red car. Colin stood still at the side of the road.

"Why aren't you racing?" asked Connie.

"I am," replied the larger cone. "I'm cleverer than he is that's all."

Kurt could see he was winning the race and started to head back across the three lanes.

**BANG!**

He was hit by the front bumper of a blue car and sent high into the air. He landed with a bump onto the tarmac of the motorway. A second car ran over him and flattened him. Then a white van knocked him onto the grass in the middle of the motorway.

"See," said Colin. "I'm just waiting until the cars and lorries have all gone before I try and cross the motorway. I'm much cleverer than he is."

When the motorway was quiet, in the middle of the night, Colin hopped all the way to where the flattened Kurt was lying and hopped all the way back.

Colin had won the race, Colin was the cleverest of all the cones, and Colin was now the leader. All of the old cones from the yard close to the M4 cheered.

The following morning when the workmen came to do their work they saw the poor squashed cone in the middle of the motorway and wondered what had happened. They waited until the road was clear of traffic and went to pick him up. It would be a few days until he could be put into the machine that mends broken cones and he could return to work.

When the workmen finished work that afternoon they collected all of the cones and took them back to the shed in the yard close to the M4 motorway. Colin climbed down from the stack he had been placed on and spoke to all of the cones inside the shed.

"From now on," he began. "Motorway cones will live on this side of the shed and all the other A-road cones can live on the other side next to the draught."

The old cones cheered.

"And I don't want any of you to ever think about trying to become the leader of our group. If you do I will beat you and you will end up in the cone hospital, like Kurt."

"If we accept that you are our leader can we please all just live and work together nicely?" asked a small shivering cone on top of a stack near the draught. "We may not be from a yard near the motorway, but we can learn how to work together."

Colin thought for a while. He didn't like the idea of having cones from an A-road in his shed. Motorway cones lived in motorway yards.

"Yes, okay," he said slowly. "But you will have to behave yourselves and learn quick."

"Thank you," said all of the cones in the draught. "We will."

And so the family of cones in the yard close to the M4 motorway grew and learned to live together.

If you ever see a cone lying squashed in the middle of the

road have a look at the edge and see if one of the big cones is smiling. If he is it may be Colin and he's just won another race. And remember the next time you cross the road, don't rush, wait until the road is clear, look both ways, listen and then look again. That is what a clever cone would do, to make sure that you don't get hurt.

# Scaredy Cones

Have you ever been to a fete or a funfair and seen orange and white traffic cones standing in lines marking the queues, or stopping people tripping over tent pegs? Have you ever wondered if they enjoy being at the funfair or fete? And have you also wondered what they got up to when all the people left? Did you think that they just stood where they were placed, or did you think that they did something completely different? Well, perhaps they do stay where they are placed and perhaps they don't.

It was a glorious hot summer morning and the orange and white traffic cones from the yard close to the M4 motorway were working at a fete in the local village. The grounds of the manor house had been turned into a fairground for the weekend. There were stalls selling cakes and jams, stalls where people could win a goldfish just for throwing some Ping-Pong balls into a bowl, roundabouts and all sorts of other rides for children. There was even a beer tent for the adults to stand chatting in while their children enjoyed the fun of the fete.

All of the cones were stood in various places around the grounds, some were stood in lines to show where the queues should be, others were guarding holes and dangerous objects, such as tent pegs, so people wouldn't hurt themselves whilst they were having fun.

Colin had been placed next to the ghost train entrance, he was stood in front of a large wooden stake which was holding up the huge banner over the entrance saying 'Welcome to the scariest ghost train in the world. BE AFRAID!' Colin wasn't afraid, because Colin was the biggest and bravest of all the cones in the yard close to the M4 motorway. The cone who was guarding the other large stake was Kurt, another large cone with a light on his head. He was almost as brave as Colin, but not quite. The two cones had spent all day watching children and their parents marching into the ghost train all excited and then coming out of the exit frightened sheet-white.

"I wonder what's inside there," Colin whispered to the other cone.

"I don't know, but I guess it's really scary," replied Kurt in a low whisper.

"What makes you think that it's scary in there?"

"All of the people who are coming out look scared. It takes quite a lot to scare people."

Colin thought for a short time then said. "Would you be scared if you went inside?"

"No," replied Kurt, not very sure of himself. "Would you?"

"Of course not," replied Colin angrily. He stood up to his full height to make himself look as brave as possible. "I am a motorway cone. Nothing scares a motorway cone."

"Nothing?" asked Kurt.

"That's right," answered Colin. "Nothing."

"What about that spider that is climbing up your body?" asked Kurt.

Colin screamed and started to hop about trying to get rid of the spider. Kurt laughed at the sight of, Colin the bravest cone in the yard close to the M4, jumping around the place scared of a little spider. He stopped laughing when he saw another, much larger, spider climbing up his orange and white plastic body.

That night when all the people went home from the fete all of the cones met in front of the big wheel and had a meeting. Colin was in charge of the meeting and said he had stood and watched all the people having fun all day and now it was their turn to enjoy themselves.

"What are we going to do?" asked Connie, one of the smaller cones. She was very excited.

"We are going to do all the things the people did," replied Colin, his orange light was flashing brightly and excitedly. "We will get some balloons and candy floss. Then we will try and win teddy bears and goldfish. We can have a go on all the rides, the big wheel, roundabouts and swing boats, and those of you who are brave enough can join me on the ghost train."

"What's a ghost train?" asked Clara. She thought the ghost train sounded very scary.

"The ghost train is the scariest train in the whole wide world," began Colin. He marched up and down in front of all the cones as he spoke. "Only the bravest cones would ever dare to enter it."

The rest of the cones gasped.

"Are you going on?" asked Kurt.

"Yes," replied Colin bravely.

"Then I think I will join you," said Kurt, puffing out his chest.

The rest of the cones gasped again. Then the whispering

between them began.

"Colin and Kurt are going on the ghost train," said one.

"I'm not. Are you?" asked another.

"No," replied the first.

"Me neither. It sounds too scary," added another cone. "I'm a bit scared of the big wheel myself."

The cones all had a wonderful time. Unfortunately they found it really hard to eat the pink and fluffy candyfloss and the toffee apples. It was also very difficult for the cones to throw the ping-pong balls into the fish bowls, which was quite good really, because they didn't have anywhere to keep the goldfish if they did win one. It would have been a lot easier if they were tall enough to be able to see the bowls they were throwing ping-pong balls at. The cones did, however, have immense fun on all the rides. There were plenty of "wee's" and "yahoo's" as they went round and round or swung backwards and forwards. All of the cones loved the bumper cars, especially when some of them stood in the middle of the floor and caused traffic jams, for the first time in their lives the cones had found out what it was like to be stuck in traffic. They all beeped their horns and moaned about the stupid cones stopping them getting to where they needed to go. It was very funny and they all had a long hard laugh about it, until their plastic sides hurt.

It was getting very late, the sky was dark, the moon was hidden behind great big black clouds, and there wasn't a single star in the sky.

"Who is coming with me onto the ghost train?" asked Colin.

All the cones fell silent, none of them were brave enough to go onto the train with Colin.

"I will!" said Kurt very bravely. He stepped forwards to join Colin on the steps of the ghost train.

Both Colin and Kurt began to shake nervously, neither of them wanted the other to know they were slightly scared. They both stepped into the darkness of the ghost train, the rest of the cones thought they looked very brave.

Colin and Kurt sat down in the train next to each other. The train started with a jolt and began clicking its way around the dark passages inside. There were squeals of witches and laughs from the vampires as the train continued on its way along the track. Coffins full of skeletons opened their lids as they went by. There was plenty more laughter from vampires and squeals from the witches. If Kurt could, he would have covered his eyes so he couldn't see all the scary things. He hated hearing all the noises of witches and ghosts and vampires. He hated it even more when cold things touched him, it made him jump.

Colin enjoyed the ride so much he was laughing back at the witches. He loved the skeletons jumping out of coffins at him, he thought they were incredibly funny. He wasn't scared by the cold things touching him as he went past, because he knew they were just bits of old curtains hung over the track.

Kurt was getting fed up with Colin laughing back at the scary things, he was so fed up he pushed Colin out of the train. If Colin liked the ghost train so much he could stay there. Colin fell out of the train and landed with a bump next to a particularly un-scary skeleton. Kurt spent the rest of the journey through the ghost train with his eyes tightly closed and trying hard not to listen to all the scary things screaming and laughing.

When Kurt came out of the exit all of the other cones were waiting for him, he looked very scared, his white bits were particularly white.

"Where's Colin?" asked Connie.

"He was so scared he got out and ran away," lied Kurt, leaping out of the train when it stopped at the station. "Now, we had better all get back to our positions ready for the people to come in the morning."

All of the cones did as they were told and went back to their positions and waited for the morning. All, that is, except for Colin, he wasn't scared in the ghost train and was thinking of all the fun he could have when the people arrived in the morning.

The following morning all of the people started arriving at the fete. The organiser moved another cone, called Clifford, from one of the lines to where Colin should have been standing. Clifford and Kurt watched all the people go onto the ghost train, they saw that, like yesterday excited children were going in. Instead of coming out as white as sheets, they were all coming out laughing.

"I thought the ghost train was a scary ride," said Clifford.

"It is if you are a scaredy-cone," replied Kurt, proudly holding his head up high.

"Why are the children laughing then?" asked Clifford.

"I don't know."

The owner of the ride didn't know either. Usually children came off his ride quite scared indeed, but for some reason today they were all laughing. He decided to go and investigate.

When the ghost train owner walked along the track into the ghost train he saw that everything was perfectly normal in the first chamber. The second, third and fourth chambers were also fine. He eventually arrived in the fifth chamber and saw what it was that everyone who had been on his ride was laughing at. One of the skeletons dancing about waving his arms in the air was wearing a cone on his head for a hat, a big cone with a flashing orange light on top of it. The man himself thought it looked very funny too. He took Colin off the skeleton's head and took him back outside where he belonged, as soon as he had moved Colin all the children coming out were all as white as sheets again, the owner was extremely happy.

"Where have you been?" asked Clifford. "Kurt said you had

ran away scared."

Colin glared at Kurt. "I wasn't scared. Kurt pushed me out of the train because he was so scared and I just stayed in there having fun."

That night, when the fete had closed, all the cones were in the back of Vera on their way back to the yard close to the M4 motorway, Colin told them all about the skeleton wearing him as a hat and how he had made the ghost train a funny place. Kurt didn't gather around and listen to Colin's story he just sat in the corner of the van and muttered under his breath, "Humph!"

The next time you go to a fete or a funfair and see orange and white traffic cones helping out have a go on the ghost train and see if you can find Colin messing about trying to stop children from being scared. If you don't see Colin in the ghost train please don't be scared by anything you might see in there. They are not scary really. Are they?

# Clever Cones

Have you ever been to school and seen orange and white cones guarding a hole or where workmen have been working? Did you think the cones were just standing there to remind you not to fall in the hole when you were playing in the playground? Have you ever wondered if any of the cones actually learnt anything while they worked in a school or if they just stood there, still and silent all day long not listening to anything going on around them? Well, maybe they don't listen to what is going on, or maybe they do.

The cones were busy guarding a hole that had been dug in the middle of the playground at the local school. None of the cones knew the reason why there was a hole in the playground, in fact none of them really cared. They enjoyed watching the children run around and play whenever the bell rang. When the children weren't running around the playground playing all sorts of games with each other the cones found that, as always, they were bored. There was nothing to do apart from watch the workmen work, very slowly and listen to the radio the workmen had stood by the hole.

"This is so boring," said Keith. "When is the bell going to ring again?"

"What bell?" asked Craig, who had been busy watching a spider try and fill his head with a web.

"The bell that tells the children to come out onto the playground and have fun," replied Keith.

"Why do you want them out here?" moaned Craig. "They are so noisy."

"Because they are a lot more fun than watching these stupid workmen do their stupid hole digging," answered Keith quite angrily.

When the workmen went back to the yard to collect some more tools and some new batteries for their radio, Keith went off in search of the children. He hopped across the playground to where the school buildings were. It was a lovely warm morning and the teachers had opened the windows of the classrooms to let the fresh air in. Keith could hear the children working and answering the questions the teachers were asking.

"What is the capital of France?" Keith heard one of the teachers ask her class.

"F," Keith answered under his breath.

A boy inside the classroom gave the correct answer, "Paris."

"Humph!" Keith said under his breath.

The teacher asked another question. "What is the capital of England?"

Keith knew the answer wouldn't be "E" this time, so he didn't even bother to answer under his breath.

"London, Miss," a young girl answered.

"Londonmiss," Keith said under his breath. "I've never heard of it. I've heard of a place called London, I've seen it written on lots of signs with numbers after it, but I've never heard of Londonmiss."

Keith soon realised that geography was not his best subject so he hopped over to the grass to stand under another open window. The subject inside the classroom was maths this time. The teacher asked questions to the whole class quickly, one after another, and the children in the room would all answer together.

"What is ten times by ten?"

"One hundred!" the class chorused.

"What is one hundred halved?"

"Fifty!" they chorused again.

"What is three times by seven?"

"Twenty-one!"

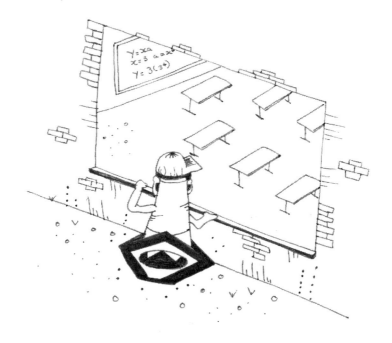

Keith huffed and puffed outside the window, he couldn't do the sums quick enough to join in the chorus of answers. The reason he wasn't any good at maths was because he only had ten fingers to help him do the sums.

After three more windows containing lessons of art, science and history, Keith stood under a window and listened to the children and the teacher saying all kinds of things he couldn't understand at all.

"Bonjour!" the teacher said.

"Bonjour!" replied the children.

"I would like you all to count from one to ten," she asked.

"Easy," Keith thought and he began. "One, two, three, fo." He stopped when he couldn't believe what he was hearing.

"Une, doux, trois."

When the children had said ten strange words the teacher clapped her hands and said, "Well done. Tres bien."

Keith was very angry now, the children had got the answer wrong and yet the teacher was pleased with their answer. In fact he was so angry he hopped back to the rest of the cones in disgust.

"Did you find the children?" asked Craig, when Keith returned. "Are they coming out to play?"

"No, they are busy learning things. Can you believe the teachers are teaching them wrong?" said Keith.

"What are they teaching wrong?" asked Craig.

"Well, they ask them questions, the children give the wrong answers and the teachers say they have done well and got the answer right," replied Keith.

Keith then told the rest of the cones about "F" not being the capital of France and all about Londonmiss. He was particularly cross when he spoke about the children counting to ten in gobbledegook. The rest of the cones couldn't believe what they were listening to. Fancy teachers teaching children the wrong things and praising them when they didn't get the answers right.

The next day when the workmen had gone off for their lunch break all of the cones by the hole decided to go and listen outside the windows to see if the stories Keith was telling them were correct. It wasn't that they didn't believe what Keith was telling them, it was just that they knew sometimes Keith liked to make things up to make things sound a little bit more exciting then they actually were.

Sure enough they stood underneath the windowsill and listened to the first lesson. Keith was right they were teaching the children complete rubbish. Everyone knows the capital of Spain is "S" it is also the capital of Sweden and Scotland. The next window they listened underneath the children were all talking in a silly language and the teacher was praising them for being so clever. The cones were outraged and extremely angry with the teachers for teaching the children total and utter rubbish. What could they do? Children would never listen to what a cone had to say. Cones were not allowed to speak in front of people they had to just stand still and guard things when people were about.

They all made their way back to the hole they should have been guarding and had a chat about what they could do to help the poor children from being taught incorrectly.

"When they come out to play after the bell has rung we could speak to them in English and count to ten for them so they would get it right the next time they were asked," said Carrie.

"We can't speak to people, we are not allowed," replied Keith.

"Why doesn't one of us go back to the yard in Vera when the workmen finish for the evening and ask Colin? He is really clever and he would know what to do," said Craig.

"No," snapped Keith. "We will not go and ask Colin, we will work this out for ourselves. We are just as clever as Colin is."

Keith stayed awake all night. He stood in the playground when the rest of the cones were sleeping and tried to think of what it was they could do to help the children. It was really dark in the middle of the playground and Keith was very tired, but he knew he had to teach the children properly and show the rest of the cones he was just as clever as Colin. Then one day, maybe, he could be the leader of all the cones in the yard close to the M4 motorway.

When the night was at its darkest Keith finally had an idea he thought would work. For his plan to work he needed the help of the rest of the cones.

"Wake up you lot," he called. "I've got it!"

The other cones slowly woke up and stretched to get the sleep out of their plastic bodies.

"What's the matter?"

"Why are you waking us up?"

"Is it morning yet?"

So many questions were asked all at once and none of them made any sense because they were all asked with sleepy voices. Keith quickly told them his plan and they all helped to put it into action. They finally finished just after the sun came up and just before the first of the teachers started to arrive at the school. Keith was very pleased with himself and the rest of the cones, they would teach the children properly and not all the rubbish the teachers were telling them.

One of the teachers walked into her classroom to set it up for the day and saw on the blackboard big shaky letters saying.

*Don't listen to teachers. Teachers are wrong. Cones are right.*

Who could have written that? She went to the next classroom and saw the same message, in fact someone had written the three sentences on every blackboard in the school. She looked out of the window into the school playground and saw the orange and white cones all stood by the hole, each one of them had a number written on them in chalk. They were all stood around the hole so the numbers counted from one to twelve. She rubbed her head and wondered who could have written on the blackboards and who would have written numbers on the cones.

When the workmen arrived at work that morning the teacher who had seen all the messages went to talk to them and she told them all about the writing on the boards and the cones.

"Why would anyone think teachers are wrong and cones are clever?" she asked.

"Teachers don't stop cars falling into holes in the middle of the road," Keith said under his breath. "And cones know how to count to twelve."

The children never did get to see any of the messages the cones had written because, the teacher had rubbed them all off before any of the children saw them. After all who would have believed that teachers were teaching children incorrectly?

Keith was pleased he had got his message across to the children and they would not listen to the teachers. He didn't know the teacher had rubbed them all off before any of the children saw them.

If you ever see cones stood in a line in your school playground guarding a hole, have a look and see if they have got numbers written onto their bodies in chalk. If they have make sure they are all lined up in the correct order and count the numbers out aloud so they can hear you. If they haven't got numbers on them count them anyway so they think they are teaching you something. And please don't do it in French or Spanish or any other language, even if you are clever enough to be able to do it, because it will just upset them.

# Emergency Cones

Have you ever been a passenger in a car along a motorway and seen lights on top of all the cones in a line? Have you noticed that sometimes the lights seem to flash in sequence and look as if they are leading the way along the road? Did you think someone had programmed the lights to flash in sequence? Or did you think the cones themselves decided when to let their light flash?

Perhaps the lights are programmed. Maybe the lights flash when they want to. It might just be possible there is a different reason all together.

It was a foggy night on the M4 motorway. It was so foggy the cones from the yard close by could only just see the cones stood next to them. They were chatting to each other to stop the boredom. It wasn't working, all of them were bored.

"I'm bored," said Keith. "Why don't we play I spy?"

"Okay," replied Colin. He paused for a moment, then after a long sigh said, "I spy something beginning with F."

Keith stared into the whiteness of the fog surrounding them. He couldn't see anything beginning with F. In fact he couldn't see anything beginning with any letter of the alphabet. "I give up," he said. "All I can see is fog."

"Well done," said Colin. "Your turn."

"But I can't see anything apart from all of this fog."

"Exactly," said Colin grumpily. "We are not going to have much of a game of I spy then are we?"

"We could have a game of football," said Clara, excitedly whilst kicking an imaginary ball into the back of a net.

Colin stared deep into the fog, even his orange light did not shine through the fog far enough to see much farther than a few metres in front of him.

"There's no point," he moaned. "We won't be able to see each other. Let alone see the goals we need to score in."

Every now and then cars and lorries would hurtle past the line of cones stood on the hard shoulder. The cones knew they were passing because they could hear them, and they could see the fog shine brilliant white in their headlights as they approached, before they saw the red glow of the backlights disappearing into the murk.

"Colin?"

"Yes, Keith?"

"Can people see in the fog better than cones?"

Colin thought for a while, he had seen some of the workmen eating carrots and he knew they made you see better in the dark. So they must make humans see better in the fog too.

"Of course they can," he replied. "Why?"

"Well," began the young cone. "If I was driving a car and I couldn't see very far in front of me, and I can't, I would be driving a lot slower than I did when I could see."

"Then they must definitely be able to see in the fog," said Colin. "If they couldn't it would be far too dangerous to drive quickly."

Suddenly away off in the distance, deep into the white curtain of fog, the cones heard a screech of tyres on the tarmac of the motorway. There was a loud bang too, followed by two more and then the sound of glass breaking.

"What was that?" asked Clara, shaking nervously from her top to her bottom.

"I think it was a crash," said Colin.

"What are we going to do?" asked Clara. "We can't see the crash."

"The drivers of cars won't be able to see the crash either," said Colin. "We need to do something."

"Like what?" asked Keith, excitedly. "Are we going to have some fun causing traffic jams."

"No," growled Colin. "We are not going to have fun, but we are going to stop more cars and lorries crashing into each other."

"Why?" asked the younger cone.

"Having fun is all right some of the time, but we do have a job to do and now is the time to do it."

Something needed to be done quickly and Colin had to think fast. The fog was too thick for the drivers to be able to see the cones white reflective covers shining in their headlights. The drivers would not be able see their orange plastic bodies either. The cones would all need to have flashing lights on their heads to shine through the fog as a warning. Colin and Kurt were the only cones with lights. Two cones with lights on their heads would not be enough.

An idea came to Colin. "Pass a message to Kurt and tell him I need him here now."

"But I don't know where he is," grumbled Keith.

"Then just tell the cone next to you to pass the message on to the next cone down the line," snapped Colin. "And do it quickly!"

Colin drummed his fingers on his folded arms as he impatiently waited for Kurt to emerge through the fog. He heard someone coming towards him out of breath. Finally Kurt was stood beside him. He leant on Colin panting heavily, he was desperately trying to get his breath back before he could speak.

"What do you want?" panted Kurt. "What's so important?"

"There's been a crash," said Colin.

"I know. I heard it." Kurt was still panting.

"We need to stop other cars and lorries smashing into the ones that could be all across the motorway already."

"How?"

"Lights," said Colin. "We need flashing lights and lots of them."

"But there's only you and me," grumbled Kurt, still panting.

"I know but I have a plan."

Colin told Kurt his plan to stop more cars crashing into the already crashed cars on the motorway.

"Do you think it will work?" asked Kurt, he had got all of his breath back by now.

"It has to," replied Colin.

Some the cones dashed off back to the yard, at least they

went in the direction Colin said the yard was. The rest of the cones formed a long line from the hard shoulder to where the cars were sitting all smashed together and steaming. Colin and Kurt were stood at the front of the line holding their lights in their hands, they waved them as hard as they could whenever a car or lorry sped through the thick fog in an attempt to make the drivers aware of the danger.

"It's working," called Kurt, holding his orange light high above his head.

"I know," shouted Colin, waving his from side to side. "But we still need more lights."

"Keith and the rest should be back soon," shouted Kurt through the gloom. He was still waving his light above his head as hard as he could.

Colin and Kurt could see a feint glow of orange light in the distance breaking through the white sheet of fog. It seemed to dance and flash through the thick cloud.

"They're back!" yelled Colin, still waving his light above his head.

"Over here!" called Kurt. "And hurry."

Keith and the rest of the cones returned to the line along the edge of the motorway, they were all carrying two orange lights, one under each arm.

"We collected all of the lights from the store shed," said a slightly out of breath Keith. "What shall we do with them now?"

"Keep one yourselves and give the other one to somebody who doesn't have one," ordered Colin like a Sergeant Major. "Then get in line."

When all of the cones had an orange light in their hands they held them above their heads, just like Colin and Kurt.

"I've always wanted a light," whispered Keith to Clara.

"Me too," she replied. "A light makes you feel so much stronger and braver."

"I know," said a third cone. "I look just like Colin now."

"Yeah, but you're still not as tall as him," said a fourth.

When all of the cones in the line had an orange light in their hands Colin barked some more orders. His orders were quite simple, when a car, lorry or motorbike approached through the fog Colin would shout, "Now!" He would then jump in the air while holding his light high above his head. The next cone behind him would jump in the air as soon as he saw Colin's base leave the ground. Each cone in turn would jump into the air holding their light high above their heads in a wave movement. Then, hopefully, the vehicles racing through the thick fog would see them better and not crash into the already crashed cars.

"Let's have a practice," said Colin. "Now!" he called leaping into the air.

When he landed he turned round to see if his plan had worked. The lights all rose into the air one by one, like a Mexican wave, Colin was sure this would stop cars colliding.

Colin was standing with his chest puffed out proudly at the

front of the line of cones. It wasn't long before he would have to put his plan into action. Through the fog he could hear the sound of an engine roaring along the motorway.

"NOW!" Colin jumped into the air. He could see the white lights shining through the fog.

The rest of the cones all jumped into the air when they saw the cone in front of them jump. The car racing along the motorway saw the orange lights through the fog flashing in sequence and pulled over to the next lane. Colin's plan had worked.

Everytime a vehicle approached Colin would shout and the cones would all jump into the air.

"This is just as much fun as causing traffic jams," said Keith in mid jump.

"I know," said Clara, launching herself into the air. "Colin always knows how to have fun."

Suddenly there was the feint sound of sirens approaching, Colin could see blue lights flashing through the thick fog.

"Now!" he called, jumping into the air. When he landed he jumped up again shouting, 'Now!"

Colin kept shouting "Now!" and leaping into the air until two fire engines a police car and an ambulance had rushed past.

It wasn't long before a message was past along the line from the crashed vehicles to Colin at the front of the line.

"The people in the cars are all safe. The police are pleased that there were hundreds of cones with lights on to warn people of the danger. It was almost as if someone had arrived before them."

Colin puffed his chest out once again, his face glowed with pride. For once he had done something good, and guess what? It felt good too.

Next time you are travelling along the motorway and you see lights on top of the heads of all the cones in a line look at them carefully. If they light up in sequence as you drive past see if they are jumping into the air too. If they are, listen very carefully and see if you can hear one of the largest cones shouting, "NOW!" just before he jumps.